I0655128

# THE POWER OF A FLOWERING CACTUS

One man's search for enlightenment through the agency of sacred sex and flowering plants

By Kama Tarumi

Filidh Publishing

# Introduction

This book is entirely fictitious in nature. None of its locations or characters is real. The potential resemblance of anything in this book to actual people or places is entirely coincidental and unintended.

The work's real intention is to narrate some of its characters' spiritual evolution as the result of poignant adventures, escapades, and experiences. And it has a higher purpose in attempting to capture transformative and transcendent personal phenomenon in the hope that readers might be inspired, enlightened or spiritually benefitted in some way.

It is not pornographic in nature--despite the fact that explicit sexuality and coarse words do appear. Sexual activity is an important part of life. It can be transformed from acts of lust into sacred experiences through spiritual evolution and the development of awareness.

The text delves into the possibility of spiritual growth through two distinct but related paths—sexual activity and connectivity to specific plants.

The author hopes that readers of this book will enjoy a good read and learn how others achieve inner liberation in unusual and creative ways.

Kama Tarumi
September 2017

# PART 1 – CLEO

# Chapter 1 ~ Sarah

Josh Dunaway's girlfriend broke up with him abruptly on his twenty-first birthday. He came home late after playing a gruelling hockey game and found her note on a coffee table beside the kitchen nook. It read:

*Dear Josh:*

*This will come as a shock to you, but I'm ending our relationship today. Your instability is driving me crazy. I want someone with a steady job and a future, and, put simply, you just don't have enough ambition for me. Sex with you is great, but not every day! You need to find a free-spirited nymphomaniac who loves your writing and your music. I'll pick up my stuff on Saturday morning, so please don't be home then. Don't contact me in any way. I wish you well in life.*

*Sarah*

To say he was devastated would be a gross understatement. They'd dated for over two years and lived together for the last nine months. His whole life revolved around her. During the time she'd lived with him, Josh took a creative writing course at Compton College and worked part-time as a taxi driver. His long-range intention was to make a living as a writer—a goal he took very seriously. He thought she supported him in this plan. Apparently, this was *not* true. To him, it seemed as though they'd been together forever. Sarah Sutherland was beautiful, intelligent, athletic, accomplished and ambitious, and he was madly in love with her. In her fourth year of Political Science at the University of Valleytown, she planned to follow that with a law degree. Currently, she worked as a legal secretary at Gerrod & Lennon—a branch of one of the biggest corporate law firms in the province of BC.

# Chapter 2 - Depressed

Deep down, Josh knew that Sarah was not a 'kindred spirit.' In fact, they really weren't compatible at all. She was bossy, and he constantly dreamt about being with someone more 'submissive' and sexually adventurous. She was a traditional thinker and usually voted for extremely conservative candidates in important elections. He, on the other hand, loved left-wing politics and off-the-wall ideas for improving society. For example, he favoured the full legalization of marijuana; she opposed it vehemently. She never did anything crazy or spontaneous—everything in her life was controlled, planned and organized with precision. She was headed towards a conventional, upper-middle-class life. There'd be two kids, a shaggy black poodle, a law practice and a white picket fence.

They argued constantly. They argued about money, sex, politics, drinking, work, and school. When she was gone, Josh found his life much more peaceful and calm. But he missed her terribly. She was stunningly gorgeous (and made all his friends jealous). She was also funny, full of energy, and the life of every party. Her scent was always alluring and full, but subtle. They did exciting things together, and everything they engaged in was extremely intense. However, there was just no balance in their relationship, no foundation of common values or dreams to build on.

On an intellectual level, Josh knew their break-up was the best thing that could have happened, but he couldn't stop thinking about her even then. He'd lie wide awake most nights craving to see her, hold her, touch her, make love to her, and just talk to her.

Once he knew their time together was over *forever*, he fell into a deep depression. He lost his appetite, didn't want to see his family, and stopped writing. He also quit playing hockey. Even getting up to go to work was a challenge. Some days he phoned in sick and stayed in bed all day.

His best friend and hockey buddy, Bruce McRae, called him and asked why he'd been ignoring all his friends.

"I'm really in a funk, my friend."

"Why?" asked Bruce.

"I can't seem to stay in relationships with women for any length of time. My girlfriend just broke up with me, and I'm going crazy. This is the third failed relationship I've had in three years."

"Just relax a bit, Josh. It's not the end of the world," his comrade replied. "Remember when you hooked up with that floozy from Florida? You thought she was sexy and smart. I knew from the beginning, she was toxic, like a stinking swamp full of Norwegian rats. When she disappeared with your MG, you were shocked. Not me."

"You have to admit she had a nice figure."

"Yeah, a blonde bombshell with no brains and a glittering heart made of tin. And you thought you'd never get over her! Two months later, she was a distant memory. Remember?"

"But Sarah's different, Bruce. She's bright, beautiful, and exciting."

"And totally conventional—you'd never have any freedom with her. You'd be kissing your creativity good-bye. Forget about her; she's not worth it. Trust me. If Sarah's so incompatible, why did you get so involved with her in the first place?"

"I'm not sure, but I think it's linked to my sex addiction."

"What do you mean?"

"I think about sex constantly and want to have sex every day. I love the bodies of beautiful women and constantly fantasize about screwing them. Haven't you noticed how gorgeous Sarah is?"

"It doesn't matter about that—the point is obvious—be happy you've gotten rid of her. Now it's time to focus on finding a sensuous chick, but someone who has the same values as you."

"You're missing the point." he countered to his friend. "I've got a character flaw and have to get rid of it. Right now, I'm incapable of having an intimate relationship with a woman."

"Relax, my friend. What you really need right now is a vacation—maybe a couple of weeks in the sun somewhere. Come on over to my place, and we'll have a beer."

Bruce lived in a run-down two-bedroom apartment on the corner of Sunrise and Oak. It was a shingled building that needed a paint job, with a flat roof and ten suites. Most of the occupants were eccentric, poor, and irritating to live around. The landlady's name was Lily Walters, and she was a bit of a tyrant.

Bruce himself was a character. He had curly red hair, a dimple in his chin and a slight beer gut. He wore gumboots most of the time. But he was full of energy, had a great sense of humour and knew how to make friends. Everyone liked him. He worked as a skilled auto mechanic at a local dealership. He'd taken some advanced journeyman tickets, and he was very well paid. Which surprised his friends because he lived so cheaply and simply—a no-frills lifestyle.

Josh had stayed with his buddy on a couple of occasions when things got out of hand with Sarah. He was a true friend and pretty much accepted Josh for who he was and what he did.

# Chapter 3 ~ Diaz

About a week after the break-up, Josh went to work at his regular job—driving for the *Yellow Bird Taxi Co*. It was an afternoon shift, a hot and humid day in August. When he reached his locker, he saw a pink slip scotch-taped to it. It read:

SUBJECT: *Termination*

REASON: *Without Cause*

DATE: *Effective immediately*

He asked the dispatcher what it was all about. She said, "I really don't know. The owner was always mumbling about your unreliability, though. Don't tell him I said that."

Josh picked up his loose toiletries and an old leather jacket he'd bought in Spain and then left the building from a slit in the back door that led to a dark side alley. He was angry, but strangely, relieved. Josh hated the job. His shifts often lasted ten hours and, unless he picked up weekend work, the money was terrible. His pay was 40% of the take, and he often sat reading Playboy magazines in his car for half his shift, or more. After each day's work, he was forced to clean up his cab and wash it thoroughly, no matter how tired he was. No one ever thanked him. No one ever appreciated him.

This was one more reason to be discouraged. He *did* have some savings but could only last without another job for about six months.

Josh hung around his apartment for two weeks, watching TV, reading, eating, sleeping, smoking, playing his harmonica, and feeling morbidly dejected. He didn't write a single word. His time with Sarah had revealed a sickening pattern. He kept failing in his relationships with women. She was the third girlfriend he'd had in three years, and none of his relationships had gone anywhere.

One morning, he saw a tantalizing ad in the *Provincial* that jumped out at him. It was a *Sun Tail* seat sale to *Palarta, Mexico,* for $475 both ways—on an open ticket.

"Maybe it's time I took a holiday," he mused to himself. "I need some time to step back and find out what my life is really all about. I might even be able to stay with Cleo for a few days."

Cleo Williams was his mother's oldest and best friend. Growing up, he saw so much of her; he called her his aunt. 'Aunty' Cleo had joined Josh and his mother on many vacations, and he knew her very well. She was most definitely an interesting character and had lived a very unconventional life. She'd been married four times, was a committed Christian, and had spent three years in an ashram in India studying under a famous but controversial guru. She'd also written a book on inner healing through tantric meditational practices.

More recently, she'd fallen in love with a Mexican musician while cruising in the Caribbean. Actually, he was playing in the band on her ship. After a whirlwind romance, they married, and she moved to Caseras, Mexico, to live with him. His name was Alexandro Diaz, and he owned a funky, pink bungalow on the rise near the inland side of town, two blocks from a long sandy stretch of pure white sand on Playa beach. Caseras is a quaint resort town fifteen minutes northwest of Palarta.

Unfortunately, Mr. Diaz, who was seventy years old at the time, died of a massive heart attack six months after marrying Cleo. She now lived alone in his fan-cooled adobe. It had an expansive patio stretching right across its entire front that overlooked a sweeping vista of the turquoise Bay of Banderas. After a relatively short period of mourning, she began to feel quite free in her new lifestyle. In fact, she never changed her surname and quickly started dating again.

She was tall and full of energy but had a contemplative side. Although she knew the seamy side of life, she was intuitive and could read the suffering in others' faces. Some said she was clairvoyant, although she never made that claim about herself. One thing was certain—she had charisma. She moved like an Egyptian Queen of antiquity and was sleek, slim, full-figured, and seductive.

# Chapter 4 ~ Contact

The next day, Josh hurriedly sent Cleo the following email–

July 15

*Cleo–*

*I hope everything's going well down under. Lately, I've been thinking about you, visualizing you relaxing and sun-tanning on an exotic white-sandy beach in front of your home in the hills. I'm temporarily out of work and thought I might take advantage of a flight sale and come to Mexico next month. If I did purchase a ticket on such a plan, perhaps I could stay with you for a few days?*

*Josh Dunaway*

Exactly forty-eight hours later, he received a reply.

*Dear Josh—*

*I'd be delighted if you flew here and you can stay with me for as long as you want. Just be aware that it's unbelievably hot in Caseras in August, and I have no air conditioning! Also, I'm working ten hours a day for a tour company, four days a week right now. I do hope you fly down here because it'd be fantastic to spend some quality time with you next month.*
*Tell your Mom I miss her and love her totally.*

*Aunty Cleo, oxo*

# Chapter 5 ~ Response

Josh thought about it for a couple more days, then drove directly to a *Flight Center* in Santac, a suburb of Valleytown, and talked to an agent. She was courteous but abrupt—telling him there were only two seats left.

"If you wanna' take advantage of this deal ya' gotta' act now." She said.

He pulled out his *Visa Gold* and paid in full. He was leaving for Mexico in three weeks! Once he got home, he sat down and wrote Cleo an email.

> *Dear Cleo,*
>
> *I've done it! I've booked a flight, and my departure date is August 15th. I'll be arriving at 10 pm. What clothes should I bring?*
>
> *Josh*

Then he sat on the floor of his suite, leaned against the faded yellow fridge, and played some old Neil Young tunes on his mouth organ. When finished, he rolled a thick cigarette using robust Black Leopard tobacco. Once it was tight and fat, he lit it up with a wooden match and starting smoking it very slowly, inhaling deeply. Soon, a reply from Cleo appeared on his laptop.

> *Josh–*
>
> *I'm delighted you're coming! Don't bring heavy clothes—just shorts and bathing suits! The temperature won't drop below 95 degrees until mid-September. I'll be waiting for you at the airport. What's your flight number?*
>
> *Love Cleo xox*

He felt a surge of pulsating energy flash through him. "This is just what I need," he thought. After pulling a pencil out of his top desk drawer, he wrote down some items under the heading,

To Do

1. Call Mom

2. Throw away all junk.

3. Give landlord notice.

4. Buy backpack.

5. Buy two bathing suits.

6. Email flight details to Cleo.

7. Sell furniture.

8. Tell friends and parents.

9. Go for beer with Bruce.

Then he quickly belted out another email.

*Cleo—*

*Thank you so much for your encouraging words. I really need this break right now. The flight number is 2138, and the airline is East Jet. See you soon.*

*Josh*

The first item he completed on his To Do list was calling his mother. She lived six hundred miles north, in Terra Village, so it was a long-distance call.

"Mom," he said, "I'm going to Mexico for a few weeks, and your best friend Cleo said I could stay with her for a while."

"You'd stay with Aunty Cleo?"

"Yes—she's always been extremely close to both of us."

"That'll be great, Josh—she'll love seeing you. Make sure you keep in touch with me while you're away. You can text or email me, and I'll get your messages right away."

"Okay, Mom, will do.

"By the way, what's going on with you and Sarah?"

"Mom, things are out of whack with her. I think we're going in different directions. Anyway, I've got to get away from this town for a while. Life here is driving me crazy."

"Don't lose that woman, Josh. She's from a good family and has her head glued on right."

"Time will tell, Mom."

"How's your writing coming?"

"Not good, Mom."

"How's your job?"

"I no longer work driving a taxi if that's what you mean. The job was boring, and there was no money in it. I had to move along."

"Oh, no! Are you broke?"

"I've got some savings, Mom, so don't worry."

"Don't forget to go to church once in a while. It'll keep you grounded and perhaps help you stay out of trouble. Maybe get you back on track with Sarah."

"I will, Mom, and I'll give Cleo your love."

"Please do. I haven't seen her for over two years. I miss her."

When Josh hung up, he felt strangely amused by his mother, mentioning the church. He'd been raised a Catholic and, at one time, took the religion quite seriously. As a kid, he dreamed of attending a good seminary and becoming a priest. In those days, he was fascinated by the mysteries of God and wanted to understand them better. He also wanted to inspire others to live holy lives and help the poor and the sick. However, as time passed, he fell away from the teachings of the church. So many things in Catholic theology bothered him—and some doctrines he simply thought were crazy.

His parents had separated five years before and had a bitter divorce. He was close to his mother but hadn't seen his father since he and his Mom broke up.

# Chapter 6 ~ Aroused

The eight-hour flight to Mexico was uneventful. All of a sudden, his plane was circling Palarta in preparation for landing. It was dark and muggy outside, but the city lights shimmered and lit up everything below. Josh could see miles of lights flashing in the blackness outside the plane window as it gradually descended.

As soon as he stepped out of the aircraft, Josh was overwhelmed by a wall of heavy, moist air that smelled like hot dried bananas. Sweating profusely, he waited patiently as the line-up snaked its way in slow motion towards the brown-uniformed, waiting custom officials, and beyond, to the exit doors. Finally, Josh found himself walking up a ramp leading to the lobby. Cleo was draped over a rail waving at him as he approached the landing. He hadn't seen her in many years, but her cheerful face took his breath away. She was a beautiful woman for someone fifty-five. Her hair was long but silvery—grey. Her skin was darkly tanned, and her white teeth shone prominently out of her smile. He felt warm and welcomed. She wore a low-cut, loose white dress that flowed almost down to her wicker sandals. Her waist was tiny, but her breasts were very prominent, and Josh's eyes fixated on them for just a moment too long. She was wearing an orchid corsage, and her scent was sweet and powerful.

She rushed into his arms and whispered,

"Welcome to Mexico—it's so good to see you."

Feeling the full warmth of her curvaceous body pressed close to him, he replied,

"Thanks for picking me up."

Now he knew for sure that Bruce was right telling him to take a vacation. In their last meeting at the *Colonist Pub,* he confided in him. Josh told him he would stay with an old family friend in Mexico and ponder on why he couldn't stay in a romantic relationship.

As soon as he touched Cleo, he *knew* this holiday was meant to happen. Somehow he'd find a way to resolve his key life issue. It was critical from his point of view.

# Chapter 7 ~ Bill

Standing right next to Cleo was an older, balding fellow, a man in his mid-sixties, who meekly blurted out,

"It's good to finally meet you, Josh!"

Cleo quickly interjected,

"Josh, this is my boyfriend, Bill Janes—we've been dating for a few weeks. He's volunteered to drive us home."

"Pleased to meet you, Bill. Cleo didn't tell me about you, but this is a nice surprise."

After walking to the parking lot, Bill opened his SUV trunk, and Josh put his two suitcases inside.

"Are those small bags all you brought?" asked Cleo.

"Those small bags are all I now own in the world, Cleo!"

The drive to Caseras followed a very busy freeway but quickly turned onto a narrow bougainvillea-lined street. Finally, Bill exited onto a dirt road that was headed toward the sea. By this time, Josh could see the ocean and hear the surf crashing against a long, pearly-white, sandy beach. Eventually, Bill parked beside a grey hotel nestled into a hill within sight of the shore. Cleo's place was up higher on the slope right next door.

"Would you like to come up for a drink, Bill," Cleo muttered as she walked beside his vehicle.

"I think I'll pass tonight. It's late, and Josh must be tired from his flight. The best thing for jet lag is to get an early night. Do you need help with your bags, Josh?"

"No," Josh replied, "I'll be fine—they're not too heavy."

Josh carried his luggage up three flights of stairs to get to Cleo's home. Once inside, he gasped at how exquisite it was. The whole front of the place was floor-to-ceiling windows looking directly onto the surf and beach. Most of the other walls were lined with bookshelves full of the most interesting titles. It was an expansive place and had crimson and brown Arabian rugs with intricate Muslim designs on every floor. Some of the windows had stain glass fixtures inside of them.

"This is such a natural, beautiful place, Cleo," Josh called out.

"Glad you like it. I guess I'm pretty lucky to have a home like this. Now follow me to the back, Josh; you've got a really nice room with a queen-sized bed all to yourself."

Josh took her lead and went with her down a long hall that had bright enamel walls. At the end of the hall was a white door.

On the other side of that door was a small but immaculately clean bedroom with a view of the mountains out back and several palm trees illuminated by focused lights in the foreground. It had a small, cedar chest of drawers that stood beside a compact closet with a bead curtain. Adjacent to the bed was a shower cubicle, a toilet, and a sink. A framed print of Van Gogh's *Sunflowers* was hanging on the opposite wall beside which was a narrow closet with several hangers.

"Make yourself at home, Josh, while I go pour us some Coronas—or would you rather have red wine?"

"No," Josh answered quickly, "a cold Corona would be fantastic right about now."

"Okay, great," she replied, "Come back to the kitchen when you've cleaned up and put your stuff away."

Josh sat on the bed and pulled out his friendly harmonica. Before he did anything else, he played some bars of Janis Joplin's *Busted Flat in Baton Rouge*. That calmed him right down. Then he sucked hard on a long cigarette. It was always good to smoke when he felt tired or anxious.

"This is going to be a fantastic holiday," he muttered to himself.

# Chapter 8 ~ Conversation

Josh put his underwear, shorts, and socks in the chest of drawers and hung his shirts and pants in the closet. He washed his face with the fresh bar of soap that was sitting on the sink. Then he dried his eyes with the red, white, and blue surf towel provided. Presently he walked down the hall and began gazing at Cleo's books.

Her titles fascinated him. There were books on meditation, yoga, tantra (the science of sacred sexuality), Christian mysticism, and personal growth. Another whole wall was devoted to romance novels and biographies. Just as he pulled down a book entitled, *The Secret* by Guru Shree Rohas, Cleo appeared and handed him a cold Corona.

"Do you want a glass, Josh?" she said.

"No, the bottle's fine," he replied.

"Okay, have a seat. I loved that tune you were playing in your bedroom. I didn't know you played a mouth organ—but *you do have musical talent*!" was her response.

"Thanks, Cleo. I've been playing around with it for a couple of years. It helps me relax when I'm upset, excited, or tense."

They sat at her dining room table—a long bamboo structure with a shiny, plate glass surface. Cleo was wearing a very thin, white T-shirt and a colourful cotton skirt, which hung down to just above her tanned knees. She was not wearing a bra, and Josh could see her brown nipples protruding conspicuously. They seemed to be erect. She smelled of Coppertone.

"How are things going with you and Bill?" Josh asked.

"He's a really nice guy, Josh, and we have fun together. I just wish he wasn't quite so self-centred."

"Where did you meet him," Josh interjected.

"He's a yoga instructor, and I was taking a class of his. He is really a wonderful teacher. One night after class, I invited him to my place for a glass of wine. I lit some candles and, after some long intimate conversations, it got a little romantic. The next thing you know, he was in my bed.

I was shocked to find out how bad a lover he was. The climax of his whole sexual act lasted no longer than thirty seconds. It was very disappointing considering he was such a fit human being."

Josh wondered why she told him that piece of news and, to change the subject, quickly asked her,

"What does he do for a living?"

"He's a government clerk who works for the Ministry of Social Development in Palarta. Makes good money and likes to travel. Actually, he's originally from Winnipeg. He came down here with his wife five years ago and stayed on when their vacation ended. She flew back to Canada, and that was the end of their marriage. He now spends six months a year here. He bought a tiny condo right in the middle of town. It's cute," she added.

"What do you guys do together?"

"Mainly walk, practice yoga, and attempt to make love. He *did* take me on one weekend trip to Guadalajara," was her terse reply. "I paid for half of everything on that vacation. Bill tends to be a bit of a cheapskate, you know."

"Does he read the kind of books you do, Cleo?"

"He focuses mainly on yoga and physical fitness, but he's a hypochondriac and is totally focused on his own health and spiritual evolution. Actually, he's a man with specific tastes. Anyway," she whispered, "I'm tired and headed to bed. I'll see you tomorrow. There are blueberry muffins in the fridge for your breakfast, and coffee will be brewing when you get up. I've got to leave at 6:30 am, but I'll be home by 5:15 tomorrow night. You can walk into town in about thirty minutes during the day and maybe check out the open markets and bazaars. Tomorrow's a special day of celebration at the *Dia del Mercado*. We can go for a swim when I get home, before supper, if you want. Oh, and by the way, we just got connected to WiFi in this part of Caseras, and there's an outlet for your iPad beside the night table in your room. Feel free to use the internet anytime."

"Okay, that'll be fine," Josh exclaimed.

Cleo leaned forward and kissed him lightly on the forehead, then turned and walked gracefully toward the master bedroom. He'd definitely felt her breasts touch his chest when she kissed him. Josh stared at her tapered back, thin waist, and bare legs as she turned away and moved across the room, as if in slow motion.

"She's very shapely for someone her age," he thought. He was embarrassed to discover that his penis had by now become engorged. "This is crazy," he whispered to himself.

Josh then walked down the narrow corridor leading to his room. He fell asleep as soon as his head hit the pillow.

# Chapter 9 - Markets

Josh slept until 10 am then slowly rose. He was groggy but found his way into the shower and stood under a torrent of hot water for twelve minutes. After that, he felt awake and full of energy. He towelled off quickly, dressed, and walked down to the kitchen.

Cleo was gone. But a big pot of hot coffee was brewing on the stove, and three fresh blueberry muffins sat waiting for him on the kitchen table. The blueberries were as big as marbles and delicious, so he ate all three muffins. Before doing that, he smeared them with margarine and Cleo's homemade blackberry jam. "How delightful," He thought.

After breakfast, Josh sat at the kitchen table for a while playing Dylan's, *Like a Rolling Stone*, on his harmonica. After playing just a few bars, he felt inspired, so he got up and decided to head into Caseras. But first, he remembered that Cleo had told him he could use her internet connection, so he sat down at his iPad to write his mom a note.

He wrote a quick message—

*Hi Mom—*

*I arrived safe and sound, and everything's going great. Cleo's incredibly hospitable and generous. She sends you her love. I'll write again soon.*
*Love,*

*Josh oxo*

He smoked two cigarettes before meandering into town, walking along a dirt causeway adjacent to the ocean. It was full of colourful stalls selling everything from trinkets of all sizes to wooden statues and fresh fruit.

At one booth, he spotted a black T-shirt with a full, yellow moon on it, casting shimmering rays along a river of blue water for sale.

"How much, Senorita?" he asked a young, female clerk standing nearby.

"Eight American dollars, Senor," she answered, in heavily accented English.

"I'll give you four dollars."

"Seex is as low as I can go, Amigo," she replied.

"Okay, it's a deal," Josh squealed as he handed her the money and walked away.

He strolled along the beach barefoot and encountered more flea market tables there. At the end of the road, he noticed a towering, medieval-looking Catholic church full of Mexican congregants.

An ongoing service was proceeding in Spanish, so Josh didn't understand a word of it. But he was impressed with the devotion and piety of the people. They knelt, sang, prayed, genuflected, confessed, and crossed themselves continually. Obviously, religion was something these folks took very seriously.

By the time Josh got back to Cleo's, supper was almost ready. Cleo had invited Bill over and had cooked lots of vegetarian chilli, green zucchinis, hot peppers, and huge brown baked potatoes. It was still warm out, so dinner was served on the deck. Cleo was wearing a skimpy two-piece bikini.

"This meal was delicious, Cleo," said Josh. "Do you mind if I have a cigarette?"

"I didn't know you smoked. Go ahead and enjoy one. Do you know how I kicked the habit?"

"No."

"I turned smoking into a meditation. By doing so, I learned to become aware of every minute act involved and how it made my body feel. In time, the desire just dropped away. But if you enjoy smokes, keep going."

"Thanks, Cleo."

"No problem," she said as Josh lit up.

"Did you go to the markets today?"

"Yes, I did. I even bought a really nice black T-shirt."

"Try it on and let me have a look," she responded.

"Okay, I'll be back in a moment," he said, "and headed down to his room."

When he got back, Bill was frowning and looking irritated, but the meal was ready, so Josh sat down beside Cleo.

"What a beautiful shirt, Josh," she said.

"Thanks, Cleo, do you like it, Bill?"

"No, not much," piped up, Bill, "It makes you look like a tourist."

# Chapter 10 ~ Conflict

After dinner and drinks, Bill said, "I'm going over to Fernando's for a drink. Do you want to join me, Cleo?"

"That's the bar on the marina, right?"

"You've got it," he said.

"Sounds like a pretty good idea," she replied, "How about you, Josh?"

"You know, I think I'll pass on that one. I'm pretty tired from all the walking I did today."

When they got to the bar, Bill bought a Corona and sat down at a table with a good view of the surf. The crashing sound of waves could be heard above the din of a crowded club.

"I'm really pissed off," Bill announced, wincing as he spoke.

"Why?"

"I think you're sending the wrong kind of messages to the very *young* son of your Canadian friend."

"How do you mean?" she replied in astonishment.

"You're dressing very provocatively in front of Josh, and it's inappropriate." Bill countered.

"Provocatively?"

"Yes, provocatively! Wearing a very skimpy bikini with loose straps is wrong. Don't you notice how Josh keeps staring at your breasts? It's embarrassing." He stammered.

Cleo frowned deeply and sat silently, drinking her beer for many uncomfortable moments. Then she looked to one side and said,

"Maybe it's good that you're going back to Canada next week, Bill. We need a break from each other."

Bill looked wistfully out to sea and then said, "Cleo, I'm really stuck on you. We've got a great thing going. When I come back, I think we should live together. It's just that you sometimes do inappropriate things. But I can live with that if you'll just tone it down a bit."

"How do you mean?"

"Josh is sexually attracted to you, and you're encouraging it. One silly move, and we'll have very inappropriate sex happening—and that's sick. You're thirty-four years older than him! Please promise me you'll be more discreet in the future."

After she finished her beer, Cleo paid the waitress and got up to go. Standing over Bill, she said,

"I'm heading home now. Let's call it a night."

Bill Janes went back to Canada the following Tuesday, and she never saw him again.

# Chapter 11 ~ Arousal

Josh spent his first weekend in Mexico on the beach. He and Cleo decided to sunbathe all Saturday afternoon. It was sweltering, the sea was glassy calm, and the beach was filled with throngs of happy Mexicans. Families with young children, teenagers with friends, and old people with dogs and cats clung to the beach or waddled into the shallow, boiling hot sea. It was a very relaxing way to spend time, even if the hordes were noisy and the heat oppressive.

On Sunday, it was even hotter. After a lunch of nacho chips, salsa, guacamole, and beer, Josh said,

"Let's lie in the sun on your deck today. I'm sick of all those boisterous kids."

"Okay, Josh, that'll be just great."

Cleo lay on her stomach beside the back wall on top of a thick foam mattress. She unbuttoned her bikini top and whispered,

"Josh, could you put some sunscreen on my back?"

"Sure," he replied.

Josh picked up a tube of *Coppertone* and squirted some onto his open palms. He then slowly began to rub the lotion into Cleo's back. He moved his hands with sensitivity and care, fully present to the situation.

After her back was fully lathered, Josh kept massaging it. He even put his hand just inside her bikini bottoms and gently touched the top of her buttocks.

"That feels fabulous, Josh. Thanks."

He pulled his rubber mattress up next to hers and lay down.

"Do you want me to put lotion on you too?" Cleo asked.

"Yes, please," he replied.

As Cleo got up, her bikini top fell onto the deck beside Josh. Her ample white breasts then swung freely in the slight, hot breeze. Her dark brown nipples were thick, taut, and hard, projecting straight into the air for a least an inch. She then began to massage his back with deep, circular movements. This continued for over thirty minutes before Cleo lay back down beside him. By this time, Josh was flushed and sexually aroused by his mother's friend.

"Did you have a lot of sex with Sarah?" she asked him.

"Not as much as I wanted. She didn't like it much."

"How long has it been since you've had intercourse with a woman, Josh?"

"It's been a long time, Cleo."

"How long?"

"A month or so…"

"That's too long to go without sex for a young man like you, don't you think?"

Josh agreed wholeheartedly.

# Chapter 12 ~ Touching

"I think it's just about time for supper, Josh." said Cleo.

"Yes—I'm getting hungry. Do you mind if I have a shower before we eat?" responded Josh.

"Not at all, dear. I'll start the meal while you go back to your room and shower."

Josh got up and sauntered down the hall leading to his room. He quickly stripped and climbed into the shower.

The water was hot, and he lathered himself with liquid Dove. Just before he turned the cold water on to wash away all the soap, he noticed a shadow behind the curtain.

Cleo slowly pulled the plastic drape open and stood before him. She was completely naked, her pure white breasts heaving and her thighs covered in perspiration.

"Can I come in?" she asked.

Cleo stepped into the shower before Josh could answer and came up very close to him. She looked directly into his eyes as she began to rub the lather around on his back. Her breasts pressed hard against his chest, and her stomach pushed up against his erect penis.

"I'd like to teach you the secrets of authentic love-making, Josh. Just relax."

Josh shut his eyes, and Cleo massaged first his back, then his buttocks, and legs. Then she reached up and washed his hair, scratching his scalp softly with her fingernails.

"Turn the cold tap on so the water will get a bit cooler, and I'll rinse you off, Josh." She whispered directly into his right ear."

The shower head sprayed water all over Josh, and Cleo used a face cloth to rinse his body off and drain all the soap away.

When he was completely clean, she reached outside the shower and picked up a colourful beach towel with pictures of sharks on it. Then she proceeded to dry him off completely. When they were both dry, she threw the towel down and pulled back up against him. She wrapped her arms around his back and stared into his eyes for over a minute. They stood there in complete silence.

Finally, she whispered,

"You're well-endowed, Josh, and I'm very experienced in the art of love. Let me teach you at least some of the basics."

Even though he felt very strange about his current predicament, Josh involuntarily stuttered,

"Oh-Oh-kay, Cl-Cleo."

He was blushing and shook all over as they stepped out of the shower.

# Chapter 13 - Love

Cleo sat down on the queen-sized bed in Josh's room and moved into the lotus position, still naked. Her skin was soft, moist, and silk-like. Her enormous breasts bounced slowly up and down when she spoke with animation, and her thin waist quivered. Josh could not take his eyes off her naked body. She was the youngest looking senior he'd ever seen. She leaned over, patted on the eiderdown, and said,

"Come over here and sit down opposite me."

"I'm feeling this is a bit inappropriate, Cleo," winced Josh.

"But you've got no idea what's going to happen yet, my dear."

Following her instructions, he sat across from her, naked and vulnerable.

"Look into my eyes, Josh."

Josh stared into Cleo's receptive eyes, feeling the warmth and compassion of an adoring woman. They sat motionless, with their eyes locked together, for ten minutes. Josh noticed how large and blue her eyes were; pure love shone out of them.

"Josh--sexuality, lust, and pornography, are *always* inappropriate. The world today is completely over-sexualized. But sex itself is very sacred when permeated with love. People today don't know anything about *real* sex."

"Exactly what do you mean, Cleo?"

I used to engage in lustful practices. I discovered sex at the age of fifteen, and I became totally addicted to physical contact with men. You could say I was a real nymphomaniac. For some reason, my genitalia was always overly sensitive. Having orgasms sent me into ecstasy for hours. I've been married four times and slept with hundreds of men.

But, when I went to India and studied tantric meditation, I learned how shallow lustful sex is. There's inevitably a hangover when it's done, and vital energies are completely drained away, not to mention the possibility of sexually transmitted diseases.

"Would you like to experience *sacred* lovemaking?"

"Are you sure it's the right thing to do, Cleo?"

"Do you love me, Josh?"

"Yes, I do, Cleo."

"Then," she whispered, "It's exactly the right thing to do. I'm going to show you how to expand the love you already have. This means love-making *not between two bodies or two minds* but between two souls. When that happens, two beings actually become one."

# Chapter 14 ~ Ecstasy

Cleo got up and walked around to the foot of the bed. "Josh, move over here and sit on the edge of the bed with your feet planted firmly on the floor."

He moved slowly into position. Cleo then raised her right leg onto the bed, reached over, put her right hand behind his back, then pulled herself up and placed her left foot behind Josh's back. She then lowered herself down onto his enlarged phallus.

Cleo's vagina was soaking wet, and she was able to easily insert his penis so wholly that his testicles touched her thighs.

"Wow, I can feel you all the way up to my stomach," Cleo winced. "Don't move, stay absolutely still. Now, look into my eyes."

Josh could hardly contain himself but did as instructed. As he gazed into her eyes, he felt calmer--but his groin was tight and in a state of intense, *red-hot* stimulation.

"We're going to move energy up your spine, Josh. You mustn't lose power by wasting a drop of sperm."

"Please let me move inside you, Cleo, please."

"Shhh. Now close your eyes. First of all, slow your breathing down. Breathe deeply but slowly, very slowly. Are you doing that, Josh?"

"Yes."

Now, visualize a ball of golden light sitting at the base of your spine. Do you have it?"

After a long period of silence, he said,

"Yes, Cleo, I see it."

"Watch that golden ball move very slowly up your spine, Josh, and get bigger as it travels. Feel the warmth and glow of its rays and feel the pure energy moving up your back with the ball."

Josh was hurled into a universe of bliss. An imaginary golden ball of light was moving slowly up his back. Soothing rays of light were emanating from it, and energy from his genitals was rising toward his head. When the ball got to his neck, he felt real warmth all over. Then it moved into his head.

"Cleo, the space in my head is lit up, and it keeps expanding."

"Stay with it, Josh. Move that golden ball in between your eyes and hold it there."

"Have you done that, Josh?"

"Yes, and I'm holding it there."

"Now watch the golden rays shine all throughout your body. What does that feel like?" asked Cleo.

"It feels like I'm looking into space at noon in the tropics. It's hot inside, but I'm calm and peaceful. My head is full of energy."

"Don't move a hair on your body, Josh. Stay with it. Now watch the rays light up the whole sky."

He was tranquil as the space expanded. The rays of golden light opened to infinity. Josh stayed motionless inside Cleo for over an hour, eyes closed, lost in his visualizations. He felt like a sizzling raindrop falling into the Indian Ocean as he finally moved out of her and eased back onto the bed, fully stretched out, in total relaxation. All of a sudden, he wasn't a person anymore, just a wave of ecstasy moving in infinite space.

# Chapter 15 ~ Peace

The next morning, rays of sunlight shone through the half-open Venetian blinds in Josh's room. They landed on his naked body and eventually woke him up.

He stood up and looked around the bedroom. Everything looked different; the room seemed bigger and much more spacious. A quiet peace enveloped him, and his thought processes had slowed to a standstill.

Josh suddenly noticed that his powers of observation were much keener than usual. The flight of a black house fly sounded like a buzz saw. The colour of hanging curtains was a much brighter crimson, and the sun's feel on his skin felt like a massage. He walked slowly over to his white underwear and put them on, moving as if in slow motion.

He sat down at his iPad and noticed an email message from his mom. He read it slowly. It said—

> *Dear Josh—*
>
> *I'm glad you arrived safely and are having a great time with Cleo. She's a wonderful person—but a bit of a non-conformist. Have you had any adventures with her yet?*
>
> *Don't forget to go to church once in a while if you get a chance—and stay in touch.*
>
> *Love,*
>
> *Mom oxo*

He felt strange hearing from his mother at that moment but stayed aware of his thoughts as he got up from the desk. He wanted to talk to Cleo about a vivid dream he'd had, so he headed down to the kitchen.

As he entered the room, he immediately smelt pungent coffee fumes, pancake syrup, and Cleo's sweet vanilla shampoo. It was a Saturday, and she wasn't working.

"Good morning, my dear," she whispered. "I've made breakfast for us—here, have a seat."

"Cleo, I had a very lucid, erotic dream last night which you were in, and now everything seems very strange. Have I landed on a different planet?"

"It wasn't a dream, Josh. Everything you dreamt about last night *actually happened*."

"Oh, my God," he replied, holding both hands over his whole face. "What were we thinking?"

"First, tell me why everything seems so strange."

"I feel so relaxed, peaceful and calm—I can't believe it. My thoughts have slowed down, and everything I see looks incredibly beautiful—even a fly on the wall."

"Last night, some of your chakras were opened, Josh. All the sexual energy you have was transformed into spiritual power. Because you were able to stay fully in the present moment and not have any kind of sexual release, your inner power was magnified. At this moment, you're fully alive and present. What you're seeing now is reality. This is how life is supposed to be lived—in peace and joy, moment by moment."

Josh sat down and poured raspberry syrup all over the two pancakes that were sitting on his plate. Then he bit into them. They tasted absolutely delicious, and he savoured each and every sweet morsel.

"This is just the beginning of your apprenticeship into *real* love-making, Josh. Soon we'll move more deeply into it."

Josh then went back to his bedroom and sent his mother the following email—

*Dear Mom—*

*Thanks for your message. I absolutely love it here in Mexico, and Cleo is an incredible hostess. We haven't gone on any trips yet because she's working during the days, and I've been busy scouting the place out. Cleo's home is exquisite and sitting in her garden is like basking in paradise.*

*I'll be in touch soon.*

*Love, Josh*

# Chapter 16 ~ Presence

The strangeness Josh felt after his exotic night with Cleo lasted powerfully for about two days and then lingered. Things moved along as usual after that, except for the fact that Cleo sometimes moved around her home completely naked.

He came in from the beach three days later, and Cleo was standing by the kitchen table without a stitch of clothing on. Her figure took his breath away. The hair on her head was silvery-grey, but her skin was soft, smooth, tanned, and supple. Her over-sized breasts hid her upper body's tapering from broad shoulders to a very tiny waist and jet black pubic hair. She was the personification of voluptuousness.

"Josh, please relax and listen to me. From now on, I want you to do an exercise the moment you feel sexually aroused in my presence."

"I feel sexually aroused now, Cleo."

"Good. Sit at the table and close your eyes. You must learn to turn lust into presence."

"What do I do now, Cleo?"

"Watch your breathing and slow it down. Your breath is critical—it's the bridge from your flesh to your spirit. Breathe deeply, inhale slowly, and then exhale slowly. Now start to count your breaths. Every inhalation counts as one. As you count, stop thinking."

"I keep having thoughts about touching you."

"Let those thoughts go and keep counting. Feel kindness towards yourself and your body. Compassion is one of the keys. I'll be back here in one hour."

At first, Josh struggled with the exercise, but he gradually calmed down and stopped thinking so much. The deep breathing relaxed him and made him calm. By the time Cleo came back, he was immersed in a cloud of tranquillity and peace.

"Are you still turned on, Josh?"

"No, I'm very calm now."

"Did you feel compassion for yourself during the exercise?"

"Yes, very much so," he responded.

"Okay, you can open your eyes."

Cleo was sitting opposite him, dressed in a long orange sari with glass beads all over it.

"Now it's time for supper," she said.

As she spoke, she removed two hot soy and tomato tortillas and a plastic bowl of cucumber chilli from the brown bag she was carrying.

"Enjoy your meal, Josh. This stuff is from a popular take-out joint just down the road."

Josh noticed that his observational powers were again heightened. The smell of the chilli was so strong it lit up his whole nose. The inside of his nostrils felt like a bonfire.

"You seem really present now, Josh."

"I am, Cleo, I really am."

"Good, I'm glad. Tomorrow we're going on a run in the mid-day sun. Then you'll become even more present. Trust me."

# Chapter 17 - Running

The next day, after a leisurely breakfast of bananas and raspberries, Cleo said, "Now it's time for a run, Josh. Did I ever tell you that I was a runner?"

"No, you didn't, Cleo."

"Over the years, I've learned that running with a certain kind of awareness melts my neurotic tendencies and makes my heart strong. I call what I do "inner running" because it's not goal-oriented. I've found that after jogging for about forty minutes, my ego drops away, and my whole being opens up to the natural world."

"I've worked-out by playing hockey and tennis but never running. And all my sports activities have been intense and very competitive." He answered.

"There's another way to approach exercise, Josh. Follow me, and I'll show you."

Cleo was dressed in shorts and a T-shirt, and so was Josh. They both had light runners on.

Over the hill behind the property, they walked out of the house to a sandy path edged by towering palm trees. It was intensely hot. They travelled along a trail that led to several sand dunes stretching to the mountains beyond.

"Take your runners off now," she ordered, "and feel the sand on your feet. As we start to run, focus on breathing very deeply. When your breathing slows down, start counting your breaths from one to ten, then back to one again. If you start thinking, just come back to your breath. When I tell you to forget about counting, start moving without effort. Then you'll be in the flow.

They started running towards the hills. Josh's feet were burning as the sun rose directly above his head. He was sweating profusely.

"Has your breathing slowed down, "asked Cleo.

"Yes."

"Are you counting your breaths?"

"Yes."

"Now stop counting and continue running without any effort."

Josh kept running and let go of everything inside his head. He could feel some pain in his back and feet, but there was a sense of peace in the desert as he moved along.

Cleo was a phenomenal runner. Her pace was smooth, and her legs moved gracefully over the sand. Josh could see the sun flashing over her outstretched thighs. He followed her and noticed she was not breathing as heavily as he was.

An hour into the run, they came upon an oasis of sorts. Actually, it was a tiny pond surrounded by several cacti.

"You look exhausted, Josh. Have a sip from my water bottle and rest now."

Just then, Josh drank a little water and knelt on the hot sand. He gazed at one particular cactus that seemed exquisitely beautiful to him at that moment.

All of a sudden, he began to merge with the cactus. Its long needles and green hew were magnificent. But most of all, he *loved its red flowers*. He felt totally at one with the plant. Then, magically, he was inside it and understood the world from its point of view. The separation between him and the cactus evaporated, and his thinking completely stopped.

"Are you alright, Josh?" asked Cleo.

He was jolted back to reality and whispered,

"Cleo, I just disappeared and became that cactus. I feel ecstatic now."

"You've had another satori experience, Josh. That's wonderful!"

"What's a satori experience, Cleo?"

"Let me put it this way—when the Buddha had his enlightenment under the *Bodhi Tree*, the veils of worldly suffering were lifted from him, and he realized directly that the source of bliss he'd been searching for all along was actually to be found within his own being. Having a satori experience means getting a glimpse of that reality."

"That makes sense—a lot of sense! Yes, it was definitely a mini satori!"

# Chapter 18 - Fasting

Over the next two weeks, Josh had very little physical contact with Cleo. Occasionally, she hugged him or gently touched his arm, but that was it. However, he was experiencing powerful feelings of love for her. In her presence, he felt happy and calm. Everything she said or did was perfection itself in his eyes. She was so beautiful and graceful.

"Now it's time for you to fast for three days, Josh," she stated matter-of-factly one Saturday morning. Then I'll show you some powerful exercises to open you up. Trust me on this."

By this time, disobeying Cleo would never have occurred to him. He'd never been this happy before in his whole life, not even as a kid.

"I'm not allowed to eat anything for three days? He queried.

"No solid foods."

It was easy for the first two days because he kept drinking mango juice. But by *Day 3*, he was irritable and edgy.

"I feel very weak, Cleo. Are you sure I should keep going?"

"Yes," she replied, "Tomorrow morning, we'll break the fast and later in the day, we'll do the exercises."

The next morning, Cleo left a note for Josh on the kitchen table. It read—

*Josh—*

*There's fruit here and juice for your breakfast. Eat only fruit today. Tonight we'll move into the exercises.*

*Love,*

*Cleo oxo*

Later that day, after a light meal of avocadoes, tomatoes and mayonnaise, Cleo put on a sixties Bob Dylan CD and turned the lights down. Josh remembered hearing the soft sounds of, *Like A Rolling Stone*, as Cleo spoke.

"Strip down to your underwear, Josh," and sit in the love seat over there."

Josh then walked across the room and sat down in a small orange love seat in the corner. Then he leaned back in a very relaxed pose.

"Good," she said. "Now completely let go of yourself and listen to my instructions."

For the next forty-five minutes, Cleo had Josh tense—then relax—his feet, knees, back, shoulders, neck, and jaw.

"I'm so mellow I could fall asleep," he murmured.

"Close your eyes and slow your breathing down, Josh," she whispered in a sultry voice. "Breathe deeply and start counting your breaths."

Cleo then went behind Josh and began massaging his shoulders. Soon, he fell into a deep sleep.

At the first light of dawn, he woke up and dressed. Slowly he walked outside into the garden. Again, his thought processes had slowed to a virtual standstill, and an envelope of peace descended upon him. Everything he gazed upon was perfect and looked intensely beautiful to him. A speckled frog croaked and jumped onto a dry branch lying on the ground. To him, it sounded like a foghorn.

"What a strange but beautiful sound that was. Everything I look at is absolutely sacred, just the way it is," he thought, "and I'm blissfully happy. This must be *another* satori!"

Josh's rapture lasted until Cleo arrived home for supper.

# Chapter 19 - Writing

During dinner, Josh started sharing some personal thoughts with Cleo. "I've started writing again," he said.

"That's great, Josh. What are you writing about?"

"First, I want to do a fictional short story about a sagacious woman in her fifties who has healing powers."

"That sounds interesting."

"Then I want to write a non-fictional manual on the plants and flowers of Mexico-with a special focus on cacti. That'll involve lots of research. But I also want it to include some actual gardening knowledge and experience."

"Why do you want to write that kind of book?"

"Because the flowers and plants down here are exquisite. They're so alive and full of exotic colours—they really speak to me, especially the cacti."

It's fantastic that you're writing again, Josh. That inspires me. But there's another topic I'd love you to research for me."

"What's that, Cleo?"

"In Palarta, there's a cathedral called the *Basilica de la Soledad*. Every second Thursday, a Carmelite father hears confessions there in the mornings. He's a hermit who lives alone in a small hut down the coast, very close to the village of Esoterica. It just so happens he's an authority on St. John of the Cross and many of the great medieval Christian mystics. He's said to have authentic healing powers. Sitting in total silence, praying, fasting and following the Carmelite Rules are some of his practices. If you could interview him, it could be the basis for another book. This man can teach you great secrets if you talk to him."

"Who is St. John of the Cross, Cleo?"

"He was a medieval Spanish mystic who was made a saint by the Roman Catholic Church. His most famous work, *The Dark Night of the Soul*, chronicles the soul's journey from her bodily home to complete union with God. The actual *experience* of God, rather than mere belief, was the goal of many of the great mystics."

"I'm only a nominal Catholic these days, Cleo, but I'd love to talk to this man. May I take confession with him one Thursday morning?"

"Yes," replied Cleo, "But first you have to make an appointment by calling Father Rios, the Church Rector. I just happen to have his phone number because I'm a member of his church."

"That's wonderful, Cleo. What an opportunity this could be."

"Yes, my love, it could be."

"You're a Catholic, then?"

"Well, let's just say I go to church sometimes and have some great contacts in the Catholic world. I may not believe in the superficial teachings. Still, I resonate with Catholic mysticism, and the lives of the saints inspire me."

# Chapter 20 ~ Mysticism

Two weeks later, on October 1st, Josh was scheduled to take confession with Father Graham, the Carmelite hermit. He arrived at the cathedral twenty minutes early and started walking around the main vestibule. On each side of the long wooden benches, squared-off sections containing colourful religious scenes were cordoned off with golden rope. One had a large statue of the Virgin Mary reaching out, while another held a desk where one of the Popes sat studying the Bible. The cathedral was immense with towering stone pillars and long diamond-shaped stain glass windows full of many of the Stations of the Cross. It was tranquil. The slightest sound echoed throughout the whole church.

At the back of the building, on the left, stood a confessional booth. At precisely 11 am its door opened, and Josh entered after hearing the command,

"Come in."

"Have a seat, Josh, and relax."

It was a dimly-lit enclosure, and Josh could just barely see the shadowy outline of a priest.

"Have you ever confessed your sins before?"

"Not since I was a child, Father."

"Do you have anything you want to get off your chest?"

Josh sat in silence for several seconds before speaking.

"Yes, I do."

"What is it, son?"

"I've participated in sexual activities with a friend of my mothers, who is thirty-four years older than me. At first, I felt tremendously guilty, but now I've justified the acts because none of them contained the slightest element of lust."

"How do you mean?"

"I love this woman, and each act of sexual contact has been absolutely sacred and pure."

"Let us pray about it, Josh," said the hermit.

"How shall we do that, Father?

"Be completely still and silent."

Josh sat in silence for twelve minutes before Father Graham whispered,

"True prayer is a deep listening—listening to your soul. Just allow everything to be as it is—and listen with your whole heart."

Josh could hear some light footsteps in the church and faint organ music in the background, but as he sat there in silence, his thinking process completely subsided. He visualized Jesus, giving the *Sermon on the Mount*, but with no words—just visual images. Finally, the hermit said,

"It's time to go now, Josh. A light lunch has been arranged in the kitchen so you can ask me a few more questions."

"But father, you haven't given me any advice."

"You don't need *my* advice. Just spend time in complete silence, and God will advise you. Trust me, when you surrender to silence, God speaks. And He speaks in his own way."

"Thank you so much," Josh replied.

As he walked out of the confessional, he noticed the father walking towards the front of the church. He moved silently and as if in slow motion. There was a grace to each one of his movements. It looked as though he were floating, not walking. His face was lit up, and he had a mysterious smile. Charisma oozed out of every one of his pores.

"This priest is a holy man," he thought.

# Chapter 21 ~ Contact

Josh watched Father Graham walk down an aisle between the seats. He followed him as the hermit descended a flight of winding stairs at the front of the church. At the bottom, the priest turned into a large kitchen where coffee and tea were brewing and fresh egg salad sandwiches, spiced-up with crisp dill pickles, had been prepared.

Josh had never seen anyone like Father Graham before. He even looked like a saint! He was tall, thin—even emaciated—yet his whole face shone brightly. He moved very slowly, and every action he undertook was mindful, graceful, and full of light.

"I understand you're a writer? He said.

"I'd like to become one, sir," replied Josh.

"Are you interested in the religious life?"

"I don't think I'm cut out for *that*, but I'd like to learn more about it and have spirituality enter my writings somehow. Can I ask you a few questions?"

"Why, of course."

"What kind of order are the Carmelites?"

"Carmelites refer to a group of religious hermits who came together on Mount Carmel in the early Middle Ages. Later, they formed an order which emphasized a life of strict adherence to holy principles. They vowed to remain chaste and poor, work endlessly, fast periodically, and pray without ceasing. They did so in order to find God."

"What about St. John of the Cross?"

"He came centuries later and, with Teresa of Avila in Spain, formed a new Carmelite Order. However, in doing so, they encountered criticism and censure. St. John was even thrown into jail--but it was there that he wrote his best book, *The Dark Night of the Soul.*"

"What is that book about, Father?"

It's St. John's instructional manual for how to achieve union with God. It's very complicated and involves many austerities and disciplines. Finally, just before the ecstasy of God is experienced, John says one must go through a period of extreme spiritual dryness--what he called a "dark night." But Josh, I can tell you the ascent to God can be experienced directly without a great deal of darkness or renunciation."

"How can that happen?"

"God is not sitting on a mountain somewhere. His presence is constant. However, human beings are too distracted, too disturbed, and too preoccupied to notice. His hand is in everything. If you can sit still and go deeper into your own being, His presence will become obvious. Then, if you dwell in that place, His nature will be revealed to you."

"What is His nature, Father Graham?"

"Peace, love, joy, happiness, beauty, and wisdom."

Josh felt overwhelmed with satisfaction and clean and clear throughout his entire being. For some reason, he asked the friar a strange question,

"Is there any way I can stay in communication with you and keep asking you more questions, Father?"

"You can email me at my address at this church, and I'll get your messages periodically when I come into the city. I *am* willing to answer them."

"Thank you so very much, Father. I really appreciate your generosity."

# Chapter 22 ~ Correspondence

"How was your visit with Father Graham, Josh?" asked Cleo that evening. "Fascinating, Cleo," he replied. "But it was so much more than his words. Just watching him and being with him had a huge impact on me."

"How do you mean?"

"He had a healing energy. When I left the church, I felt so alive, healthy, and vibrant."

"That's amazing, Josh," Cleo responded. "Do you think you might write something about him?"

"Maybe, but I'm actually more interested in writing about you! But he did say I could continue to communicate with him via email."

"I hope you won't publish anything controversial about me."

"Don't worry; you'll be concealed in a story."

"Are you going to follow-up on the Father's offer?"

"Yes."

Josh sat down later that same night and composed a note to the hermit. It read,

> *Tuesday, October 1*
>
> *Dear Father Graham—*
>
> *I'm writing to thank you for your generosity in being willing to spend time with me and answer my questions.*
>
> *I found your words very inspirational and hope to communicate with you on a regular basis.*
>
> *Sincerely,*
>
> *Josh Dunaway*

Exactly two weeks later, he received a reply.

Tuesday, October 15th

*Dear Josh—*

*Thank you for your kind words. I enjoyed meeting with you on October 1st.*

*It has occurred to me you might want to visit my hermitage and study with me for a period of time. Before you rush to respond, please consider that most of my days are spent in prayer, contemplation, and physical labour.*

*May God bless you and lift you up.*

*Father Graham*

Josh was shocked to receive this invitation from such an elevated spiritual master. His first reaction was to pass up the opportunity. He thought the discipline would be too hard for him. But upon further reflection, he began to see merit in spending time with the friar. Maybe it would lead to significant personal growth? That evening, he asked Cleo,

"Father Graham has invited me to study with him at his hermitage—do you think I should go?"

"Absolutely, Josh—you *have* to go! Chances for spiritual growth like this don't happen very often in life."

The next morning, Josh wrote back to the priest.

October 16th

*Dear Father Graham—*

*Thank you for your response to my message. I've given your proposal some consideration and have decided to take you up on your offer. I'd love to spend the month of February at your Retreat, if at all possible.*

*If this can be arranged, please let me know what I should bring with me when I come.*

*Most sincerely,*

*Josh*

Here was the priest's reply—

Tuesday, October 29th

*Dear Josh—*

*Yes it would be possible for you to join me in my spiritual studies for the month of February.*

*Here's a list of the things you'll need to bring:*

*Change of clothing*
*Pair of gloves*
*Pad of paper*

*I look forward to seeing you early next year.*

*Peace,*

*Father Graham*

At that point, Josh sent an email to his mother. It read—

*October 29th*

*Dear Mom—*

*I'm having a wonderful time in Mexico! Two weeks ago, I spent time with a Christian mystic who has now invited me to spend the month of February at his hermitage. I'd be studying religious texts and doing spiritual exercises.*

*Cleo thinks this would be an excellent opportunity for me. I hope you agree. The teacher's name is Father Graham. Please don't be put off that he's a monk. The important point is that he's a very wise and holy man.*

*We're thinking about you and hoping all is well.*

*Love,*

*Josh oxo*

# Chapter 23 - Love

During the month of November, Cleo periodically slept with Josh. When she did, she wore no clothes but instructed him *not* to touch her. However, she sometimes massaged his chest and thighs.

"It's important that you contain your sexual energy and not release it under any conditions. Then the passions you experience will drive up your spine and open all your chakras."

"What happens when my chakras are all opened, Cleo?"

"You'll begin to experience yourself as pure energy and enter states of bliss. The boundaries that cause you to feel that you're a separate self will begin to dissolve. By December, I'd like you to be ready to make love to me for three hours without ejaculating."

"Then what will happen?"

"If you're lucky, you'll have a *major* satori."

By this time, Cleo and Josh had become very close. They spent every non-working hour together. They talked endlessly, swam, ran, hiked, shopped, and ate together. They were very compatible and inseparable.

Sometimes Josh knew what Cleo was thinking or what she was about to say before she even opened her mouth. In her presence, he felt at ease, happy, ecstatic. He couldn't admit the truth to himself because Cleo was so much older than him. Still, the truth would have been obvious to even the most casual observer—they were in love. They touched each other lovingly, frequently, and hugged at the slightest provocation. Although Josh was sexually attracted to this much older woman, there was purity in their relationship because it was permeated by a profound sense of love. Occasionally Josh would spontaneously kiss Cleo passionately on the mouth as their tongues became one. Those kisses sometimes lasted for minutes, and Cleo never resisted them or pulled away until Josh was completely finished. All she ever asked of him was that he never release any sperm. She wanted him to continually drive his sexual energy upward.

# Chapter 24 ~ *Kundalini*

On the 4th of December, Cleo told Josh she'd be attending a Meditation Group the next night.

"Some good friends of mine meet once a month for a session of meditation, Josh. We're having a meeting tomorrow night. Would you like to join us?"

"Sounds like a great idea!"

The next evening, after supper, they left Cleo's place and walked into town. Halfway up a side street, she turned right and walked fifty paces. Josh followed closely behind. She stopped and knocked on a red, wooden door with the number 757 on it.

"Good evening Cleo. I'm glad you could come tonight. And who is this good looking young man beside you?"

"He's the son of a good friend, Carol, and he's been staying with me while he vacations in Mexico. His name is Josh."

"Well, hello Josh, I'm glad you joined Cleo tonight. Come on in and make yourself at home. Choose any seat you want."

There was soft Beatles music playing in the background. Four other women sat in the lotus position on an orange carpet in the middle of the floor. Musk incense filled the room, and large, fluffy cushions lay all around the edges of the carpet.

Josh sat down beside a long shelf full of books and quickly glanced at some of the titles. Most of them were written in Spanish.

"Before we get started," Carol noted, "I'll light all the candles."

Just then, Josh noticed candles placed strategically all over the place, some tiny, others round or square mounds of coloured wax, with protruding white wicks.

"Could you pass me that box of *Red Bird* matches, Josh?" asked Carol, as she pointed to a small box with sandpaper sides, sitting on a coffee table.

Josh picked up the box and slowly passed it to Carol. She gently took it from him and, ever so slowly, opened the box, took out one pine stick and ran it across one of the box's sides. Brief flashes lit up the room as she walked around, lighting all the candles. The smell of hot sulphur permeated everything.

"Let's start with fifteen minutes of silence, folks," she said. "When the joint gets to you, take a puff on it, but only if you want to. It's not necessary for our purposes."

Josh felt serene when the marijuana cigarette was passed to him. He briefly glanced at Cleo, who was sitting across the room, and she smiled as if to say, "Go ahead," so he took one short pull on it. Then he passed it along.

Josh could see that Cleo also took a puff as they sat there in total silence. When it came around to him again, it was almost burnt-down. He took one last drag on what was left.

After that, they stayed in silent meditation for over an hour, breathing calmly and deeply. Finally, Josh opened his eyes. Everyone in the room was sitting silently, and all was calm. The whole scene appeared immaculately peaceful and tranquil.

When they got back to Cleo's place, Josh felt very hungry. But, more than that, he was happy, calm, and a bit high.

"Now it's time for you to make love to me with everything you've got, Josh. You're now fully prepared for ecstasy. Come into my bedroom and take off all your clothes. I want to look at you."

Josh sauntered into Cleo's room. Only a night light was on, so it was dim, but he could see her body in its nakedness. She was radiantly beautiful. Her white skin glowed in the dark, breasts swaying slowly from side to side; her thick pubic hair the only shadow.

"I can see you're ready for this. Josh. I've never seen your penis so hard."

Cleo moved under the covers and motioned Josh to join her.

"Lie on your back and just relax, Josh. Let me do all the work."

Cleo started massaging his chest, ever so slowly. Gradually she worked her way down to his loins and slowly stroked his phallus.

"I'm going to put that generous member of yours into my mouth, Josh. Don't release any sperm, stay still and concentrate on your breathing. I know this may be difficult, but it's your final test."

She moved down slowly and eventually put her mouth on his rock-hard penis, using her tongue to massage him as she moved her mouth up and down his shaft. At one point, her lips touched his testicles. His entire phallus was in her mouth.

After sucking it for about ten minutes, she pulled her mouth off and moved her legs over his stomach.

"I'm very horny and aroused, Josh. *But you must stay calm.* I'm going to make passionate love to you but don't come, no matter what. You can do this. There's so much at stake here."

With that, Cleo mounted Josh and let his member penetrate her so that his balls hit her thighs.

"Now pump me, *bang me hard,* Josh. I'm going to have an orgasm, but don't let it throw you off. Count your breaths. Visualize the golden ball climbing your spine, spraying light everywhere. Stay alert, no matter what happens around you."

She then moaned loudly, and Josh could feel her juices showering his dick. He lay there with every part of his body motionless except for his rock hard cock. He concentrated on his breathing and the ball of golden light moving up to his head.

"Now that I've come, I want you to stay inside me for at least an hour, Josh. Please concentrate. If I have another orgasm, don't let it affect you."

Not long after, Cleo gasped in ecstasy. "Keep moving Josh, I'm coming again."

Josh was in a deep state of meditation when he felt Cleo's ejaculate pouring over him again. Twenty minutes later, it happened again.

Two hours later, he began to feel sleepy. He was still hard inside Cleo. By this time, he'd watched her come three times all over him. Her fluids had streamed down onto his stomach and legs. But he still hadn't released any sperm.

Suddenly he felt a massive wave of energy surge from the base of his spine up through this entire body and out of the top of his head. He started to shake all over, and his body tensed. As Cleo withdrew from him, he totally relaxed. Then another surge of energy went through him, and he shook all over and tensed again before letting go. This happened four times. Each time he surrendered totally to what was happening. Finally, he came to his senses and realized intense feelings of love spread out over his entire body.

"Cleo, my whole body is lit up inside, and I feel love welling up and pouring out of me. What just happened?"

By this time, she had her kimono on and listened to him intently.

"I think you've just had a kundalini awakening, Josh."

"What's that, Cleo?"

"I've never had the experience, but others have told me that universal life energy flows through one's entire being so that the fullness of spiritual reality can be experienced—and then expressed. Instead of breaking your energy by draining your sexual passion, you've created a circle of love within your own being. You'll never be the same again."

# Chapter 25 ~ Integration

The first thing Josh noticed the next morning was the sound of birds. They were so loud, *ca-ca-ing* continuously. He didn't remember hearing these audacious songs before.

Cleo was sipping dark roast coffee at the breakfast nook when he entered the kitchen. "How did you sleep last night, my darling?"

"Beautifully," replied Josh, "But now I'm going to take my coffee outside and sit in the back yard garden. Will you join me?"

"Yes, I will, of course," was her unhesitating answer.

Josh pulled a deck chair up beside Cleo's and noticed a vibrant green, very tall cactus in the adjacent garden. He began to stare at it.

"I never noticed this plant before, Cleo, and yet it's so beautiful."

Apparently, this delicate cactus was emanating a friendly vibration because even Cleo felt it.

"It's a gorgeous being, true enough."

"This is heaven for me, Cleo. The song of the birds, the fresh smell of the plants, the flowering cactus, and the hot sun make me feel as though I'm in paradise."

"You are."

At that moment, Josh felt happy and peaceful, utterly content with the world exactly as it was. He glanced over at Cleo's sparkling skin, lightly tanned thighs, and silver hair. She, too, was smiling.

He walked over to her, bent low, and slowly started kissing her mouth. His tongue slipped into Cleo's mouth, and her tongue met his and welcomed it. He briefly moved back and undid her bikini top, then watched it fall aside.

"Will you take your bikini bottoms off too, Cleo?" he asked her. I love staring at your natural body.

"Of course, dear, and why don't you strip too?"

Cleo and Josh necked and massaged each other for a long time before Josh asked her if he could lick her vagina, which was by then soaking wet.

"Yes, yes you can," she whispered as she threw her head back and opened her lower body.

Josh then knelt down and inserted his tongue deep into Cleo's mound, licking very hard, swallowing her juices as they came out.

"Keep going, Honey. Don't stop—but stay contained yourself—your spiritual progress depends on it."

Cleo then had an explosive orgasm and expressed herself with a series of ecstatic moans. Waves of pleasure poured over and through her body, undulating in a way that almost knocked her out. After her explosions passed, she told Josh to kiss her some more, to kiss her until she felt his love in every pore of her body and soul.

Two hours later, they paused and began to talk, maintaining constant eye contact.

"I'd never have known what real love is if I hadn't come to Mexico, Cleo. If I could hold on to this blissful state forever, I'd be totally fulfilled."

"You can, Josh. You really can."

Later that day, Josh noticed an email reply from his mother on his iPad.

December 5th

*Dearest Josh—*

*I'm glad you're having such a grand time in Mexico. I just knew you and Cleo would hit it off.*

*Studying with that monk sounds interesting but don't get too fanatical. Just going to church on Sundays is enough. But I guess studying religious texts won't do you any harm.*

*Thanks for staying in touch—I do love to hear from you.*

*Mom oxo*

Josh replied immediately. At first, he was irritated with her remarks about religious fanaticism, but he quickly calmed down and felt a wave of compassion for his mother arising inside him. He knew she loved him unconditionally.

December 5<sup>th</sup>

*Mom—*

*Thanks for your note. I can promise you Father Graham is not a fanatic—he's a saint! You'll just have to trust me on that one.*

*Cleo is a fabulous hostess. I'm so glad I took this vacation. Right now, it feels like I could move here. The country and its people are wonderful. The weather is amazing, and the flowers, shrubs, and trees are incredibly beautiful.*

*Talk soon, love,*

*Josh oxo*

# Chapter 26 ~ Demands

Two days before Christmas, Josh received a communication in the mail which was to permanently change the course of his whole life.

When Cleo got home from work, she said,

"Josh, you've received a letter. I think it's from your ex-girlfriend. Was her name Sarah Sutherland?

"Yes, it was, Cleo," replied Josh in amazement.

Sure enough, Sarah's full name stood predominantly in the left corner of a long business envelope, addressed to him. Josh tore open the contents and read,

December 18th

*Dear Josh—*

*I hope you're having a wonderful vacation in Mexico—things are pretty hectic right now for me.*

*The first thing I want to say to you is, "I miss you." When I broke up with you, I was really depressed for many reasons which I won't go into now. At the time, I didn't realize how much I loved you. But now I do!*

*I'm happy to tell you I'm six months pregnant with your child and it's a girl.*

*Unfortunately, my Mom and Dad are extremely upset. I moved back home in the summer, and things were going quite well, although it's never easy to live with parents once you've tasted real freedom. But now the situation has worsened with them; in fact, it's very tense right now.*

*As you know, they're very religious and are demanding that I get married to the baby's father. Josh that means they're insisting that **we get married** as soon as*

*possible. They're also enraged that I'm going to have to put my law career on hold indefinitely.*

*Please send me an email once you've digested the news in this note.*

*I love you,*

*Sarah oxo  ([sarah.sutherland@ craw.ca](mailto:sarah.sutherland@craw.ca))*

"Cleo, this can't be true. Sarah Sutherland says she's pregnant with my child, and her parents are demanding that we get married. She broke up with me six months ago, but it seems like six years ago now. This is an impossible situation. I used to be attracted to her, but I've moved on. The only woman I ever want to live with is you, Cleo, and I mean "forever" when I say that. Is this possible? What I'm saying is that I want to marry you. *Will you marry me?*"

"Oh my God, Josh. This does seem a bit bizarre, to say the least. One thing's for sure—you must take some time to meditate on this whole situation before making any decisions. It'd be foolish to react quickly without properly considering all the facts."

"But one thing is absolutely certain."

"What is that?"

"I love you, Josh."

# Chapter 27 ~ Decisions

Over the next two days, Josh went on three long runs, ate very little, and spent an excessive amount of time sitting beside a *Nopalitos* cactus in Cleo's back yard. He marvelled at the patterns of its deep red, flowering, *Nopal* fruit. It was stunningly beautiful, and he was transfixed by it.

On Saturday, he slept all night under that very cactus plant, drawing inspiration from it. In the morning, Cleo came up to him in the garden and said,

"Would you like some coffee, Sweetheart?

"Yes."

As he sipped his hot drink of java, ever so slowly, he began to speak.

"Cleo, I'm madly in love with you—but I've decided to go back to Canada to sort out the situation with Sarah."

"That means you'll be giving up your chance to study with Father Graham, then," she replied.

"Yes, it does."

"Then you must write to him and let him know."

"I will, Cleo. I will."

"Is this what you really want to do, Honey?"

"No, I want to marry you and live with you as your husband for the rest of my life. I love you more than words can say," responded Josh as he looked longingly at her. Their eyes locked for what seemed like an eternity before a tear formed in one of Cleo's eyes, and she turned away.

"I adore you, Josh and marrying you sounds delightful. I'd love to be your wife and dote on you forever—to cook for you, make love to you every single day—and I would want your manhood inside me *at least once* every day—take care of your all your needs and love you unconditionally. We both know that's impossible. Can you imagine what your mother would say if I married you? We'd be tormented by the world."

"No, I can't imagine what my mom would say, and I wouldn't care if we were tormented. But right now, I must do the honourable thing and sort this issue out. Can you understand that?"

"Yes, of course, Sweetheart," she stated as she stroked his arm lovingly. "When do you plan to go back?"

"In about two weeks, Cleo."

Josh then went into the house and wrote Sarah a letter. It read,

Boxing Day

*Dear Sarah—*

*I received your letter three days ago and must say its contents came as a shock to me. I never dreamt, even in my wildest dreams, you'd ever want to get back with me. I hope your sentiments don't spring entirely from the fact that you're pregnant with our baby.*

*I'm thrilled at the prospect of becoming a father, even if it seems to be happening before I'm ready to assume that kind of responsibility!*

*As you know, I'm unemployed—trying to become a freelance writer. That's my hope anyway.*

*I'm coming home to meet with you. It's my intention to resolve any issues between us to our mutual satisfaction.*

*I Will let you know when I'll be back, but it won't be long—I'll see you before the end of January.*

*Josh*

His mind was confused, so he went back outside into Cleo's garden and sat down beside the grove of green and red cacti. He noticed waves of stillness emanating from them. Then he pulled out his harmonica and played the John Denver tune, *Leaving on a Jet Plane*, over and over again. Doing that most definitely cleared his mind.

# Chapter 28 ~ Changes

On December 27th, Josh sent out two emails. The first one was to Father Graham.

December 27th

*Dear Father Graham—*

*I write to inform you how thankful I am that you've invited me to study with you at your hermitage. Being with you for the month of February would fulfill my heart's truest desire.*

*However, I've just received news that a former girlfriend is pregnant with my baby. She wants to get married as soon as possible.*

*I'm not sure if that is the best way forward for me, but I must go home to sort it all out. This means I'll be unable to come to stay with you in February.*

*I offer you a full apology for this cancellation of plans but do pray you'll understand.*

*I hope we can continue to communicate via email.*

*Most sincerely,*

*Josh Dunaway*

The second email was to his mother.

December 27th

*Dear Mom—*

*I'm writing to tell you that something shocking and amazing has just happened. My ex-girlfriend has just informed me that she's pregnant and that I'm the father of the baby. Apparently, her parents are insisting we get married before the baby is born.*

*I don't know how all this is going to proceed or end, but I have decided to fly home to sort it all out. I'll be back in Canada before the end of January. Don't worry about anything.*

*Time heals all wounds. Love,*

*Josh*

On New Year's Day, Josh received a reply from Sarah in the mail. It read,

January 1

*Dear Josh—*

*I don't know why you didn't sign off with the word 'love' in your letter to me. Do you no longer love me? I'm still in love with you.*

*Thank you for agreeing to come home. I dream daily of living with you again. I yearn to kiss you and hold you tightly. I desperately want to fall asleep in your arms! Please hurry home!*

*You're going to love our baby. It's constantly kicking now. Did I tell you I had an ultrasound and found out it's a girl?*

*I know you'll adore her.*

*Josh, I love you with all my heart.*

*Sarah*

*oxoxo*

Josh put the letter down and looked up at Cleo.

"She says she loves me. She says she's having a girl. I can't believe this is happening."

"Do you love her, Josh?" replied Cleo.

He paused for a minute to think about that question and then answered,

"I used to feel love for her, but now I realize how shallow it was. We're so incompatible! We've got entirely different world views. Besides, now that I've spent time with you, I know what *authentic* love is. It's you I love Cleo—with all my heart. After being with you, how can I ever love another woman?

"It's true, darling, the love we now have will never diminish—no matter what happens. Are you still sure you want to go back?"

"I don't know if I can marry Sarah, but I do know that I have to go back."

"I'm going to miss you terribly, Josh, but I'll stay in constant communication with you via email. My life will be completely empty without you, but I understand why you're leaving me. It's the right thing to do. But maybe I could come to visit you once the baby is born?

"Now that sounds like a fantastic idea, Cleo—I hope you do."

# Chapter 29 ~ Regrets

Over the next few days, Josh started to prepare for this trip home. On January 5th, he received a reply from his mom. It read—

January 4th

*Dear Josh—*

*I don't know why you signed off, 'Time heals all wounds,' in your note. Do you consider having a baby, a wound?*

*I'm delighted that you're coming home and that you're going to be a father. Once two people have a child together, their problems tend to evaporate over time. It's a bond between two people that can never be broken on the spiritual plane.*

*From all I know about Sarah, she's a wonderful girl. You're actually a fortunate man. I'll be in Valleytown when the baby is born. I wouldn't miss that for the world.*

*Love,*

*Mom oxo*

In mid-January, he received a reply from Father Graham.

January 15

*Dear Josh,*

*I received your message yesterday and went into a deep meditation before answering.*

*Your decision to go back to Canada is a noble one. Although I'm disappointed you won't be joining me for spiritual studies in February, I'm happy about the wonderful new developments that are occurring in your life.*

*Remember to find time to be alone, silent, and humble before God. Then true directions will be revealed to you.*

*You are most welcome to continue communicating with me via email.*

*In the Spirit of Christ,*

*Father Graham*

# Chapter 30 ~ Good~Byes

On January 18th, Josh and Cleo took a cab to the Palarta International Airport. They sat in the back seat of the vehicle, holding hands. Very few words were spoken on that trip. As they approached the terminal, Cleo stroked his right thigh with care and passion.

Just after Josh checked-in, and before he stepped on the escalator leading to Departure Bay 37, Cleo looked adoringly at him and whispered,

"The last few months have been wonderful, Josh. I feel closer to you than to anyone else on the planet. I've never loved a man as I love you. And my answer to your question about marriage is, "yes"—if things don't work out with Sarah. Remember to focus on transforming any lustful feelings you have by driving your sexuality up the spine to your crown chakra. If you do that, satoris will continue to occur, and your ability to stay present will grow. Here's a *Bon Voyage* card for you with a poem inside that came straight from my heart."

As he sat in his window seat on the plane, Josh could see Cleo leaning over a rail waving at him. Her eyes were full of tears, and so were his. As the plane took flight, he read her poem.

*Light, peace and*
*Love*
*entered my life when you arrived.*
*Your youth, beauty and*
*Joy*
*moulded me into something precious.*
*Hold my soul*
*close,*
*and be true to yourself.*
*Transform any inside baseness*
*into pure peace.*
*Shut your eyes and*
*feel my presence*
*always,*
*and my love*
*forever.*

His heart was full of love for Cleo, but there was sadness hidden somewhere inside his being. For some strange reason, he had the thought, "I don't feel I'll ever see her again."

# PART 2 – SARAH

# Chapter 31 - Arrival

Sarah was waiting for Josh at the Valleytown International Airport. The plane arrived on a cold, blustery day. There was snow on the ground outside, and the wind was icy. She rushed into his arms and hugged him tightly.

"My God—you're huge, Sarah!" he exclaimed.

"Yes. I'm huge with your baby! Put your hand on my tummy, and feel her for yourself."

She opened her coat, revealing a patterned maternity dress with pink flowers and white baby rattles on it. Josh placed his right hand on top of her dress, just before a cold wind blew her coat flaps up.

"Can you feel her moving?"

"No."

"Well, you *will* soon, she's very lively! Can we go for coffee on our way home? We've got so much to talk about."

"Okay, sounds great," replied Josh.

When they entered the Starbucks at the corner of Carnation and Jasmine Streets, Josh noticed a long line up.

"Shall we wait, or do you want to go somewhere else?" she asked.

"Let's stay here—go find a seat, and I'll order. What do you want?"

"Just a decaf coffee with no sugar—sugar's bad for the baby."

"Okay," he said.

When Josh sat down, Sarah started talking excitedly.

"My parents say you can stay at our house until the wedding. They're even going to let us sleep together in the same bed—the one in the basement guest room.

"Sarah, we haven't even discussed marriage yet, and we need to do that. The last time we had any contact, you were breaking up with me. Besides, I've already arranged to stay with Bruce for a while."

"Josh, how could you? That's not right. Having a baby changes everything, and getting pregnant made me realize how much in love with you, I really was. I want to have *your* baby and no one else's. We should be living together now. Please don't leave me high and dry. I'm sorry I broke up with you—it was a bad mistake."

"I accept your apology. There'll be lots of time to talk and work things out, and I'll only be staying at my friend's place for a couple of weeks. I also need some time to get to know your parents better before moving into their home."

"Okay, but no longer than two weeks. I'm begging you!"

"Don't worry, after two weeks, Bruce will be driving me crazy. He's a fabulous friend but *living with him* will be a challenge."

# Chapter 32 ~ Bruce

Bruce continued to work at Dutton's Auto Dealership. He also worked part-time pumping gas at a local *Starfish Station*. He'd met Josh in a history class back in his university days. It was an in-depth study on the settling of the Canadian West. They'd been best friends for years.

His apartment was shabby but practical. The rent was cheap, and the location central. You could walk to the downtown core in twelve minutes from his place.

By the time Sarah dropped him off, it was late—perhaps 10 pm—but Bruce was waiting up for him.

"You can sleep on the hide-a-bed in the TV room," he said as Josh entered his ram shackled abode.

"That's great, pal," Josh replied. "I'm only going to be here for a few weeks anyway."

"How do you feel about becoming a father?"

"Buddy, I'm confused about it. On the one hand, I'm looking forward to the experience, but on the other, I don't feel ready for all the responsibility. It seems like this is happening way too soon in my life."

"What about Sarah? Do you *really* want to marry her?"

"No, I don't. She's beautiful, popular, smart, and the life of every party—but we're totally incompatible."

"How do you mean, specifically?"

"She's conventional, straight, and not very deep. You know it already—she'll want to live in suburbia and own a house with all the accoutrements that go with modern middle-class values. That means I'll have to generate a ton of money just to keep her afloat. I want to be a writer. It may be ten years of grindingly hard work before I make a penny, if then—it's dicey."

"What are you going to do?"

"I don't know, Bruce, I don't know. Do you have an internet connection? I need to use my iPad for a minute."

"Sure, it's right beside the TV, and I've got an open connection. Go ahead and plug in."

Josh quickly composed a note to his mom and sent it.

*Dear Mom—*

*You'll be happy to hear I arrived home safely and Sarah was at the airport to pick me up. She looked great—but very pregnant—and seemed happy to see me.*

*I'm temporarily staying with Bruce, but Sarah's parents want me to move into their place. Apparently, they want us to get married as soon as possible.*

*I'll let you know what transpires.*

*Love,*

*Josh*

Then he pulled out his mouth organ.

"Bruce, do you mind if I play a tune before I hit the sack?"

"No, go for it."

He played Dylan's, *Blowin' in the Wind* a few times and felt very peaceful. Then, after smoking a heavy cigarette, he went to bed, thinking…the answer *is* blowing in the wind.

# Chapter 33 ~ Dinner

The next morning, after a breakfast of cinnamon flakes with raisins and cream, Josh caught a bus to Walmart and bought two pairs of slacks, some new underwear, and a pair of black slip-on shoes. He also activated his cell phone. Not soon after, it rang.

"How are you, my love?" I hope you slept well because I sure didn't. You just won't believe how uncomfortable this pregnancy is getting. I'm always nauseous and exhausted. Can you come to supper tonight? My parents want to talk to you."

"Sounds good, Sarah, but is it going to be a real heavy scene? I know they're not too happy with the way things are going right now."

"Everything will be fine. Just bring some flowers and your best behaviour. We're having stew and potatoes. I can't wait to see you."

Just then, Josh noticed that his mother had responded to his email.

*Dear Josh—*

> *I'm glad you're home. It sounds like Sarah is delighted with her pregnancy and, at the same time, completely **in love with you**. Those aren't bad components for marriage unless you don't love her.*

> *To be honest with you, I'd be delighted if you got married. Your child would be my first grandchild, and I'm ecstatic about that.*

> *Please stay in close contact with me. I had a note from Cleo yesterday, and in it, she said she really enjoyed your visit. She thinks you're a real gentleman, a man with character—an advanced soul.*

> *Love,*

> *Mom oxo*

Josh's reply was brief—

*Dear Mom—*

*I think I **do** love Sarah but worry about our many differences, and I don't know her family very well. But that's going to change soon. I'm going to have dinner at her parent's house tonight, and of course, Sarah will be there.*

*I loved my visit with Cleo, too. She's an amazing woman.*

*Josh*

# Chapter 34 ~ Mingling

Josh took two buses to get to the Sutherland residence. They lived in a two-story, white-stucco house in a modest neighbourhood. Except for the shrubs and bushes surrounding the house, it was quite ordinary. But all along the front and sides of the property were luxuriant lavender plants, yellow marigolds, deep green parsley, purple sage, and various types of mint.

"Someone in this family loves plants and flowers," thought Josh as he rang the doorbell, "and they know what to plant that deer won't touch."

Sarah's father, Tom, opened the door and greeted him with enthusiasm.

"C'mon in, son," he said, "we're glad you could make it."

Tom Sutherland was a balding man in his fifties with a potbelly and large hearing aids hanging off each of his ears. He worked as a real estate agent for a large, successful company. Once they arrived in the kitchen, Josh saw Sarah, her mother Ruby, and brother Samuel. Ruby was a thin woman with steel granny glasses sitting on the tip of her nose and gray hair done up in a bun. Sam was a fifteen-year-old jock wearing a black tracksuit with yellow stripes.

"Hello, Mrs. Sutherland," Josh chirped, "are you the one who does the gardening around here?—the flowers are stunning!"

"Well, thanks, son. I do like to grow a few shrubs now and again. After years of trial and error, I've finally figured out what plants and herbs to cultivate that the deer won't touch. But please just call me Ruby from now on."

"I'm impressed, Ruby. That's a great way to avoid deer eating your plants without killing anything. Here are a few red carnations to put on the table for supper, and a bottle of Merlot to whet your appetite."

"Dear Lord, the flowers are gorgeous—thank you so much! As for the wine, I appreciate your generosity, but we don't drink alcohol in this family, so you might as well take the bottle away when you leave." The tone of her voice revealed a slight irritation.

After a few minutes of small talk, Ruby invited everyone into the dining room. A large pot of beef-barley stew sat in the middle of a long, teak table. There were also a tray of fresh crusty rolls and a large bowl of bright orange, steaming carrots.

Josh sensed some tension in the room as he ate.

"That's an inspiring picture of Jesus on the wall," he said, to break the silence.

"Thanks, Josh," said Tom, "We follow the exact teachings of our Lord and Savior in this family. We believe the Bible is the word of God." After a long pause, he continued, "What kind of work are you going to be seeking?"

"Well, my long term plans include becoming a writer but, for now, I'm going to go back to driving taxis."

"What kind of writer do you want to be?"

"I was hoping to become a novelist."

"Forget about that, Josh, there's no money in writing novels. And by the way, do you have a car for your job search?" questioned Sarah's father.

"No, I'll have to start saving for one as soon as I begin working."

"My brother just moved to Toronto for two years and left his Volkswagen beater in our yard. We keep it insured and licensed as a third vehicle. You're welcome to borrow it until you and Sarah get established in your own place."

"That'd be fantastic," replied Josh, "Thank you!"

"As for a wedding, that is, if you're planning marriage, we attend a lovely Pentecostal church. It'd be perfect for a family-oriented ceremony. But we really should book it soon because this is a busy season for weddings."

After another period of awkward silence, Josh said,

"As soon as Sarah's maternity leave expires, and she goes back to work, we'll be able to rent a nice apartment."

"In the meantime, you can stay with us. We've got a spare bedroom and a tiny kitchenette in the basement."

Later that evening, Josh stood on the porch, saying goodnight to Sarah.

"I didn't know your parents were *that* religious, Sarah?"

"Don't worry, I'm not that strict!" she replied as she nestled up to him and looked deeply into his eyes. "I wish we could screw tonight, but I'm just too pregnant to make love right now. But will you please kiss me?" Their lips met, and Josh held her, his hands tightly clasped behind her back. Her perfume was exquisite. He'd forgotten just how good she smelled and how physically beautiful she was. Her sumptuous breasts pressed hard against his chest, and he felt her nipples hardening. They became long and tight against him. Her eyes met his in a longing gaze.

At that moment, all he could think about was Cleo. He wished it was her that he was about to kiss.

"I'll call you tomorrow," he whispered into her right ear, then pecked her left cheek lightly. After that, he bounded down the steps into the night.

# Chapter 35 - Reflections

When Josh got back to Bruce's place, he found his friend asleep. He quietly opened his iPad and found two new emails on it. The first was from his mom.

*Dear Josh—*

*I hope your meeting with Sarah's family went well. I dreamt about you last night. In my dream, Sarah had identical twins, and you adored them. They both came to your wedding, which was in a huge cathedral full of happy people. The only strange thing about the dream is that the officiating priest was a dinosaur! Don't know what that means.*

*Love you,*

*Mom oxo*

That email made him uneasy, so he opened the one from Cleo.

*My Darling—*

*I miss you terribly! My place is quiet, and I'm lonely right now. Some guy from work is hounding me, but I just don't feel like seeing anyone right now. Don't know why. Ever since you left, I've been feeling sad, even depressed. I can't tell you how happy I was when you were here. I've had a few dates, but all have been unsatisfactory.*

*I visualize your gleaming naked body constantly. I dream of making love to you every night and ache to touch you in sensitive places. If you were here, I'd tell you my body was yours whenever you wanted it. I'd be your slave. I crave your beautiful penis and those symmetrical testicles that hang between your legs.*

*But my real hope is that you're containing your spiritual energies and spending time in contemplation. That's how you'll keep life flowing.*

*Give all my love to Sarah and her family.*

*Yours forever,*

*Cleo oxo*

*PS That red-flowering cactus in my garden has been withering since you left. What did you do to it, anyway?*

Josh then had an overwhelming urge to contact Father Graham. He wrote—

*Dear Father Graham—*

*I'm feeling sad right now that I'm not studying with you on the coast of Mexico. But I have some questions—*

*My life is quickly heading along the path of marriage and family, but I'm still full of doubts. How can I get clarity and know the best way forward for myself and the others in my life?*

*Lately, but only occasionally, I've been experiencing feelings of peace and tranquillity—especially around plants, herbs and flowers—and some people. Then, all of a sudden, a great distraction or temptation comes along, and I'm thrust into unconscious behaviours resulting inevitably in heavy bouts of guilt and suffering. How can I stay calm and centred when these distractions arise?*

*The woman I truly love is not the woman I'm marrying.*

*Sincerely,*

*Josh Dunaway*

Then he turned to a fresh page and new file in his computer and started writing. The title he'd chosen for his first novel was, *Mystic Woman*. He smoked as he contemplated it. After staring at the title and a blank page, he lay down and started humming Simon and Garfunkel's, *Sounds of Silence*. Soon he was fast asleep.

# Chapter 36 ~ Employment

It took Josh three days to find a job. The whole process of searching for work had become much easier with the use of a car. He went to two taxi companies' offices with no luck but found success at the third—the *Valley Taxi Corporation*. They offered him a temporary, full-time position for ten months because one of their senior drivers had gone on maternity leave the day before. However, the job was Wednesday to Sunday from 5 am to 5 pm, a total of sixty hours per week. This meant he'd have to work every weekend for at least ten months. Sarah wouldn't like that, but he felt he had to get working, so he signed on.

He had a quick supper with Bruce on the day he was hired. They ate pork and beans from a can with boiled wieners smothered in Heinz ketchup.

"Let's go to the *Colonist* to celebrate your employment, buddy," said Bruce after their meal.

"I'd like to, my friend, but I've got some writing to do tonight. I want to finish some stuff before this day's over."

"Okay," he replied, "I guess you want to work on that novel you're writing. But I'll be hoisting a drink or two in your honour. If you finish your work early, come down and join me."

"I'm facing writer's block with the novel and don't know why. No—I just have to send off some emails. But if I finish quickly, I'll come down and join you."

The first bit of writing he did was respond to his mother's email.

*Dear Mom—*

*Parts of your dream make absolutely no sense to me. I can understand the cathedral full of happy people, but am mystified by the identical twins and dinosaur priest. Oh well, it was just a dream.*

*But one thing is for sure, if and when I do get married, **you've got to be there**!*

*Josh*

Then he replied to Cleo's note.

*Dearest Cleo—*

*So great to hear from you! I think you're wise not to date some thug from your work at this time. This might be a time for you to spend time alone to consolidate your energies.*

*As for my sexual energies—they're definitely contained right now. Sarah's informed me that there'll be no sex until at least a month after the baby's born.*

*Can you figure out a way to visit Canada in the near future? My heart aches to see you again and see you naked. Were you to become my slave, I'd be ecstatic. If I were living with you, I'd make love to you twice a day—and somehow manage to contain my seeds—at least some of the time.*

*Love Josh oxo*

As he sent this email to Cleo and turned to attempt some novel writing, he noticed an incoming note from Father Graham.

# Chapter 37 ~ Soul

*Dear Josh—*

*You ask me how to experience clarity in your life and stay calm in the midst of temptations. There's only one way. That way is to purify your soul. To do that, go to an isolated place for two hours every day, preferably when you're tired and hungry. When you're alone and sure to be undisturbed, close your eyes and cut off all contact with the world and with your senses. Try doing this in a sitting position. Become still and experience total silence. As time goes by, pain will arise, and you'll become very uncomfortable, both physically and psychologically. Don't escape it! Transfiguring your life will take time; how much time depends on how sinful you've been in the past. But remember, the sin and the temptations are not separate from you. They're blocked energy stored from traumatic and painful experiences you've had in the past. In silence, listen with your whole being for the word of God. Your soul will have to endure some trials.*

*In your meditations, visualize yourself entering a medieval castle. Pull the draw bridge up behind you and walk into a long stone hall. You are now completely cut off from the world. Notice that there's a large room on the left side of the hall and four jail cells on the right.*

*Imagine that each cell holds a beast. Use your imagination to picture those beasts. I'll give you some examples of how this could look. You might see a beautiful, but vicious, male tiger having sex with a black female panther in the first one. Perhaps an enormous pig with beady eyes would be munching on corn and wallowing in the mud in the second. In the third, a crocodile with ugly scales might have a large Norwegian rat in its mouth. In the last one, you could see something like a fat sloth climbing in an apple tree—searching for rotten fruit. These are your demons, and they can get out of the 'cells' under certain conditions. If you meet any of them in the castle, don't attack it and don't run away. Just be still, look directly into the eyes of the specific beast and emanate feelings of love and acceptance for that particular ghoul.*

*The room on the left has a sign above the door. It reads,* **Solitary Confinement.** *Enter that room. Climb down the ladder at the back of this space and sit in darkness in the corner. Don't let the blackness scare you. Be still and wait. Your job in this room is to completely eradicate all of your ambition. That means losing every desire you have to achieve anything or get anywhere in the world.*

*There'll be more instructions in my next email. For now, get started working with these spiritual exercises, and*

*Peace be with you,*

*Always,*

*Father Graham*


The email from Father Graham shocked Josh and strangely inspired him.

"I've got to find an appropriate place for my contemplations," he thought to himself.

# Chapter 38 ~ Homecoming

Sarah moved ahead quickly with plans for a wedding. "I've booked the church for March 14th, my dear," she said to Josh, "and I've got a guest list of sixty people—all friends and relatives. Now you need to add some names."

"Well, I've got two friends in town and my mom in Princeville. And I'd really like my mom's friend Cleo to come, as well."

"What about other relatives, Honey?"

"I've got a few cousins but don't think any of them would come even if I invited them. Our family's just not that close."

"Josh, aren't you excited? I can't wait 'til we're married and have our own little family. What about you?"

"Yeah, it'll be great," chimed in Josh.

"My parents have got your room all ready. I'd like you to move in this weekend. My folks won't like this, but I'm going to sneak into your bed in the middle of the night. We can't have intercourse right now, but there *are* things I can do to pleasure you. I'll do anything to make you happy—as long as it doesn't compromise the baby."

"Okay, I'll move my stuff this Saturday. Maybe we can go to a movie afterwards to celebrate?"

"That'd be fabulous; I can't wait."

Josh looked at his fiancé. She was dressed in a bright red maternity gown that showed her fullness. She was stunningly beautiful, but for some reason, he no longer felt that she was sexually provocative. "How can I not be overjoyed?" He thought, "I'm marrying a gorgeous, full-figured woman, and her family loves me. They're supporting us to the hilt. Why do I still feel a sense of dread about the future?"

# Chapter 39 ~ Prayer

Josh moved into the Sutherland's residence on Valentine's Day that year—it was a Saturday. He arrived at their place with his iPad, two suitcases holding all his worldly goods, and a large, green plant.

"Where did you get that huge cactus, Josh? It's almost four feet tall."

"Oh, do you like it? I bought it at a garden store yesterday and was hoping to put it in my room."

"Well, sure, if you want. Are you going to look after it, though? I'm not very good with plants."

"Yes, of course," responded Josh. "I love plants—and especially cacti. Their beauty mesmerizes me. All they need is a bit of plant food and some water once in a while."

Later, he discovered a cellar at the back of the basement. To enter it, you had to open a wooden trap door in the concrete floor and descent down a ladder to the canning racks and floor below.

"Sarah, would you mind if I hid out in the cellar occasionally? You know how I need times to be alone and quiet to recharge myself."

"That won't be a problem, Josh, as long as you don't touch anything on the shelves. We call that space the bomb shelter."

"I'll never touch any of the foodstuffs, my dear, and that's a promise."

"Okay, great."

A contented smile opened up on Josh's face. He'd found a perfect place to work on his spiritual exercises.

"Why don't you hit the sack, Honey, and I'll sneak into your room in a few minutes, and I won't be wearing any clothes."

"Sounds wonderful," he replied.

A few minutes later, Sarah slid under his covers. Even though she was completely naked, he was not in the least aroused—until she started massaging his penis.

She then climbed up on top of him and looked down at his chest, feeling his muscled shoulders.

"Massage my breasts now, darling," she whispered.

Josh stroked her oversized breasts slowly. They were pure white with rigid, brown, thick nipples. After a while, he started kissing them, and Sarah moaned with pleasure.

She then slowly slid off him and began to stroke his penis with her right hand, clasping it tightly and moving quickly up and down it. Josh's member was soaking wet, which made her hand very messy.

"I wish you could enter me, Josh."

He tried to remember Cleo's instructions to hold back the intensity he felt in his lower body. He visualized that Cleo was beside him, which made him smile. He wished she were here right now because he yearned to talk to her.

All of a sudden, he had an explosive orgasm squirting oceans of white, hot sperm all over Sarah's bare stomach and breasts.

"Oh my God, he moaned, "that was amazing. Thank you."

"I'm glad you liked it, Honey."

"But you got no pleasure out of it, Sarah." He whispered.

"That's not a problem right now because I'm too focused on the baby. It's so wonderful to hold your dick again. Next time I'll suck it and swallow your whole load. I promise."

Josh rolled off the bed and entered the en-suite, jumping hurriedly into the shower. After cleaning himself thoroughly, he dried off and slipped back into Sarah's bed. She was fast asleep by that time. He felt empty, sad and tremendously drained. He'd had a momentary shot of pleasure, but he knew the price had been high. A great deal of his vital energy had been spilt.

Then he looked back at Sarah's golden hair and clear, flawless complexion. She was exquisite in her deep sleep, but her beauty didn't stop Josh's dread and guilt. He was actually feeling clinically depressed.

"Do I really love her?" That was the last thought he had before falling into oblivion.

# Chapter 40 ~ Dread

Josh woke up in a cold sweat. It was 5 am. "Oh my God, he thought, "I'll be exhausted today if I don't get more sleep."

But he couldn't sleep. He lay there, listening to Sarah's deep, rhythmical breathing. Finally, he got up and tip-toed out of her bedroom. Shortly, he found the trap door and opened it, descending quickly into the Sutherland's bomb shelter. Sitting on a stool in the corner, he closed his eyes and took a deep breath. Once the light was switched off, it was pitch black.

He visualized entering a medieval castle and cutting himself off from all external contacts. He saw himself in *solitary confinement* and just sat there alone—still—with his back erect and feet on the cool concrete floor. He remembered the words of Father Graham, "…eradicate all ambition…" and embraced the silence—falling back into his essential nature, as Rumi had advised, "…down and down and down in ever-widening rings of being." Eventually, a picture came into his mind. It was a huge bull having rough sex with a cow, and the cow was not enjoying the ordeal. "Oh my God, that's my sex demon," he thought. "It's out of control." With a huge effort, he tried to accept that bull and generate feelings of compassion for it. Slowly, that animal backed off and meandered away from its victim.

Suddenly he felt waves of sadness overtake him. He saw himself as a frustrated father, continually arguing with Sarah. In this reverie, he'd gained weight and become sloppy and miserable.

"This is not the path for me," he realized.

Pulling out his mouth organ, he quietly played the chorus to *Hey Jude*, over and over again. "I'd sure like a cigarette about now," he thought.

Just then, he saw the trap door move and heard Sarah's whisper.

"Josh, are you down there?"

"Yes, I am," he muttered.

"C'mon up now—it's time to go to work. You're spending too much time down there these days."

He shuffled towards the ladder, immersed in dread.

# Chapter 41 ~ Compassion

Later that evening, after a long trying day at work, Josh sat down at his iPad and composed a note to Father Graham.

*Holy Father,*

*Recently I've found an ideal place for my contemplations—the dry, cool cellar where I'm now living. The Sutherlands call it their 'bomb shelter.' This morning, I did the solitary confinement exercise and found it anxiety-producing—but profound. I encountered my sexual demon—a massive black bull—and was able to feel compassion towards it, which did help matters somewhat. But just as I entered a space of utter peace within myself, I was overcome with thoughts of dread and regret about my upcoming wedding.*

*Is this a sign I should call the whole thing off?*

*On the positive side, I'm attracted to isolation and meditation—it's so peaceful when I'm all alone and quiet! But these days, my silence is continually disturbed by negative thoughts and fears.*

*I eagerly look forward to your advice.*

*Sincerely,*

*Josh Dunaway*

*PS  I pray all is well with you, Father.*

After writing this email to his spiritual guide, Josh snuck into Sarah's room and climbed into bed beside her. She was again, stark naked. He turned and started stroking her right thigh with an outstretched hand. But his head was embedded in one of her pillows, and he soon fell into a very deep sleep. He didn't even hear her whisper, "I love you, Josh."

# Chapter 42 ~ Persistence

Josh woke early, jumping out of bed at the first hint of dawn. He looked over at Sarah as he quickly got dressed.

"My God, she's beautiful," he thought as he watched her head and golden hair move on the silk pillow.

He was surprised to find a reply from Father Graham in his in-box.

*Dear Josh,*

*Thank you for your note and greeting. I'm well and enjoying the burning sun of Mexico these days.*

*It's encouraging to hear you've found a place to meditate and pray, and I'm pleased that the solitary confinement exercise is working for you. Keep doing this exercise, and when you see the bull again, work hard to befriend it. Miracles await you.*

*Should you call your wedding off?*

*The truth of the matter is—**it doesn't matter.** All that matters is staying in contact with the Holy Spirit. Stay in silence as much as you can and work on your exercises. Then you'll experience the beauty of life in whatever shows up. It's one thing to talk about God and spiritual themes, but it's an entirely different phenomenon to actually stay with Him in your experience throughout the day. For example, a marathon runner can study and read regularly about running, but unless he actually **runs**, he'll never be successful in a race.*

*The formula for abiding happiness is very simple—Stay in touch with God. To do that, you have to pray. To pray, you must become quiet, absolutely quiet throughout your whole being and then listen with all your heart. Then, be patient. God is not in a hurry at times like this. He'll guide you, and you'll feel his presence. Persist.*

*Love and blessings,*

*Father Graham*

\

Then he noticed an email from Cleo.

*Dearest Josh—*

*Things are not going well for me right now. That guy I told you was bothering me actually broke into my place last week and sexually assaulted me. It was horrible. But I screamed and kicked him in the balls before he could rape me. Then I called the police. The man is now in jail, but I feel so insecure.*

*I don't think I can ever love a man again after being with you. Everything seems so mundane, static and hopeless. I constantly wish I'd married you, but now it's far too late. I crave your youth, passion, spirituality, charisma and charm.*

*Maybe I'm just in a black mood right now. Don't take this message too seriously.*

*I adore you and dream about making love to you in a sacred way, every day— with pure love permeating my every pore. No man will ever satisfy me the way you do because you complete me physically, emotionally **and spiritually**. I feel lost.*

*Cleo*

Josh immediately answered Cleo's message.

*Darling Cleo—*

*Please don't despair. The incident with that rapist was only a fleeting experience. You are such an incredibly beautiful soul; I know you could love a thousand other appropriate men. If you are patient, the right match will come along. Trust me.*

*I wish you could come to my wedding. I won't feel fully supported without you— especially now that mom can't attend due to an injury.*

*Stay calm and know that I love you beyond words and any worldly considerations.*

*Josh*

*OXO*

# Chapter 43 - Perfection

Josh and Sarah were married on the 14th of March. It was a large affair, held in a cavernous church and attended by a room full of evangelicals, all dressed to the nines. The bride wore a long white gown with an expanded stomach to hide the baby she was carrying.

The pastor was a traditional Pentecostal clergyman and admonished them sternly to stay faithful to each other, "…in sickness and in health…'til death do ye part,…".

To Josh, the ceremony was sombre, negative, even melancholy. Throughout the service, he kept his stare on the lush green cactus he'd placed beside the pulpit. He'd been taking care of it for a while, and it was beginning to flower. Small crimson-tinged buds had appeared on it. They alone inspired him on that day.

He didn't notice Sarah's radiant face and beautiful smile—not even when he bent to kiss her just before they were pronounced, "man and wife." He didn't notice the magical stained-glass windows or the foot-long candles burning along the bannisters in front of the choir loft. He didn't even notice the wooden statue of a transfixed Christ hanging from the ceiling.

He was devastated that his mother had shattered her left leg the week before. Therefore, she was laid up in the hospital had been unable to attend—and he was still confused and full of doubts about his future with Sarah and the Sutherlands. But most of all, he missed Cleo and wished she were there to support him.

After the service, the married couple were sprinkled with confetti and whisked away to the Church Hall, where a series of celebratory events took place. The only person at the reception from Josh's side was his best friend, Bruce.

Once the speeches were made and good wishes relayed, a hearty meal was served during which booze flowed freely. The only testimonies Josh remembered were telegrams from Cleo and his mother, both read by his new father-in-law.

*To: Josh and Sarah*
*From: Cleo*

*I'm so sorry I couldn't be here with you tonight, Josh and Sarah. All my love and good wishes to a very deserving couple. May your life together be filled with joy and happiness.*

*To: Josh and Sarah*
*From: Elizabeth Dunaway*

*My heart pours out continual strands of love to you both. As I lie here in pain, I think of nothing but the joy you two will share over a lifetime. It heals me and makes me happy.*

A live band provided loud traditional religious and folk music that created a mood of abandonment and release mixed with free-flowing alcohol. The liquid consumption that night facilitated a definite increase in uninhibited behaviour.

Later in the evening, Josh danced with Sarah's sixty-year-old aunt, who pressed her enormous breasts tightly up against him. His activated penis touched her protruding pubic area as it rubbed him powerfully.

"Your manhood is impressive, my darling," Mimi whispered into his left ear. Josh smelt the whiskey on her breath and realized she could hardly stand upright. "I'd love to kiss it, Honey, and wish it well on the journey it'll take later tonight."

Although he was overwhelmed by lust, triggered in part by the four brown ales he'd imbibed, he remembered Father Graham's words about his demons. And he remembered the black bull and how he'd tamed it with compassion.

"Mimi's flirtations have activated the sex-starved bull," he thought.

"Mimi, can we go outside on the patio and talk?"

"Yes," she stuttered.

They sat down at a long table, and Josh poured both of them cups of steaming hot, green tea.

Then he stared into Mimi's eyes with a feeling of intense love and compassion. He accepted her without judgment despite her absurdly, inappropriate behaviour. They fell into a deep silence, which eventually produced several gigantic tears in her eyes.

After what seemed like hours, she gasped, "I love you, Josh, and wish you total happiness with Sarah." Then she got up slowly and staggered off—disappearing into a group of people standing around a majestic oak tree.

Josh became very still and quiet. All of a sudden, everything slowed down, and his thoughts stopped. He looked out over the party and saw everyone as overjoyed. The moon behind the patio and the waving trees beside it beckoned to him. He knelt before the cactus (which he'd brought over from the church) and closed his eyes. Waves of bliss flowed throughout his entire body. After what seemed like an eternity, his thoughts slowly came back, and he said to himself,

"Oh my God, I've had another mini-satori. The world is perfect just the way it is."

Then he noticed the cactus buds had been opening, and bright red flowers were emerging. It was spring!

# Chapter 44 ~ Suicide

On the morning after their wedding, Josh was woken by a sharp poke in the ribs.
"Josh, your Mom's on the phone crying hysterically."

"What is it? Mom, what's the matter?"

Through gasps and stutters, he heard the hesitant words, "she's killed herself...she's dead..."

"Mom—for Christ's sake, who's dead?"

"Cleo," she whispered, "I can't talk anymore; I'll call you back later."

Josh was stunned and, holding his head with both hands, screamed, "No, this cannot be."

But it was. Cleo had been found on her bed with a blue face. When they pumped her stomach out at the hospital, over fifty sleeping pills came out. It all happened the very night of his wedding, and the police report ended with the words, "Foul play not suspected."

Her funeral was to be held in five days.

Josh lay in bed all that day, crying continually. Later, as darkness fell, he said to his wife,

"We've got to go to Mexico for Cleo's Celebration of Life, Sarah. Why don't we honeymoon there?"

"I'd love to come with you, Darling, but we just can't afford it. You'll have to go alone. I'll phone tomorrow and book your flight. What's your credit card number?"

# Chapter 45 ~ Celeste

Sarah drove Josh to the airport two days later. It was dawn when they arrived, and a hazy white sun was just arising. After checking in, she hugged her husband tightly—tears streaming down her cheeks.

"I know you have to do this, Honey, but please hurry home. Our baby is coming soon, and I need you here when she arrives."

"Of course, I won't be gone long, Sarah. Thanks for being so understanding. I was very close to Cleo, and she meant a lot to my mother and me. I have to be there when they send her off."

Josh got to his seat on the flight ten minutes before take-off. After putting his flight bag in the overhead compartment, he prepared himself for a long flight. The plane was completely full except for the aisle seat beside him. Just before the stewardess started making her announcements, he noticed a tall woman strolling down the aisle towards him. She was stately, thin and agile with supple curves and pert breasts the size of perfectly round grapefruits—protruding from under a tight white sweater. A leather coat was draped over her right arm. Soon she was standing beside him and turning to sit down--after putting a small night bag under the vacant seat.

"Hi, my name is Josh Dunaway. Let's hope we have an uneventful flight."

"Yes."

"What's your name," he whispered.

"Celeste Dhaliwal."

Josh was pleasantly surprised that a gorgeous East Indian woman would be sitting beside him for eight hours. A short smile came over his whole face.

Her scent was subtle but alluring, and she had long, black, full-bodied hair that bounced when she turned to look out the window. Her skin was a beautiful brown colour highlighted by bright red lipstick that had been applied skillfully. Her eyes were as black as the ace of spades.

"I'm going to the funeral of a very good friend," he said after the plane was air born. "What about you?"

"I'm on a three-week vacation in Palarta. Ten days of my time will be spent in a Vipassana Retreat.

"Oh, really," replied Josh, "What's a Vipassana Retreat?"

It's a chance to live the monastic life for a short period of time. I'll be silent during the entire Retreat. All the participants continuously meditate from 4 am to 9 pm—except there are short breaks for light vegetarian meals. I'll observe my breath for 3 days and my body for 7.

"Oh my God, Celeste, that sounds amazing. I'm so interested. I have a Carmelite teacher who guides me on meditation, prayer, and transformation. I'll be spending some time with him on this trip.

"That sounds awesome," replied the mysterious woman sitting beside him. "So you're interested in meditation too, then?"

"Yes, I am Celeste. I'm very interested in it."

# Chapter 46 ~ Descent

By the time they flew over Kalanda—two hours into the trip—Josh realized he'd met a kindred spirit. Celeste had a magnetic personality and was passionately interested in matters close to his heart.

"Do you find contemplation helpful then?" she asked.

"Yes, I do, I really do. Unfortunately, I seem to be distracted from intense meditation quite a bit these days."

"Why is that?" she asked.

"Well, I just got married, and we're expecting a baby this month. My wife is very demanding right now, and I'm working sixty hours a week in a shitty job. Actually, I'm supposed to be on my honeymoon right now—but I had to attend this funeral."

"You know, I find contemplation is extremely helpful. When I take the time to sit in silence with specific questions I pose to myself, everything seems to work out nicely."

"Can you be more specific?"

"Well," replied Celeste, "I look at a question such as *Why does that news broadcast upset me?* Just letting the question percolate within me is how I start the contemplation. Then I withdraw into a deep silence, not doing anything. Eventually, insights arise in consciousness. It's that simple."

"So it's a process of inner, silent listening?"

"Yes—a deep listening with an unknowing attitude."

Josh's face lit up. "That's the kind of approach Father Graham has spoken to me about."

"He probably attributes the insights to the Holy Spirit, but to me, those kinds of insight just flow to me through the agency of infinite consciousness when I'm properly attuned."

Just then, an announcement was made over the plane's PA system. "Please be seated, do up your safety belts, and prepare for our descent into Palarta. We'll arrive at the landing dock in 18 minutes."

As the jet's front end dipped, Celeste became tense and shut her eyes tightly.

"Are you okay?" asked Josh.

"I think so, but could I hold on to you while we go down?"

"Sure."

Celeste then put her right hand inside Josh's left thigh and squeezed hard. Later, when he thought about it, he was sure he remembered her briefly stroking his leg. He recalled that because her touch sent electric shock waves of pleasure up and down his entire body. In all the tension of landing, Josh was fearless. His only emotion was intense sexual arousal.

# Chapter 47 ~ Contacts

Celeste stood up quickly, put her dark leather coat on, and prepared to de-plane as soon as the seat belt sign went off. Josh followed her all the way out and beckoned to her as she reached the foyer.

"Do you have time for a coffee?"

"No, I'm sorry, but a friend's waiting for me, and he'll be worried because we did arrive late."

"Well, I hope you have a fabulous Retreat, "he answered. "Can I call you when I get back to Valleytown? I'd like to follow up on any spiritual insights you might have had."

"Yes, most definitely, and I hope the memorial service goes well. Here's a business card with all my contact information. After sliding Josh the card, she turned and disappeared immediately into a moving throng of restless travellers.

Her card face read—

---

Celeste Dhaliwal

Massage Therapist and Spiritual Counselor

(email) dhali@ymail.com

(phone) 250-777-6500

---

As he looked up from her business card, he saw her coat swirl around and vanish. He then paused for a minute to think about his experience of her. "What an incredible woman—I know I'm going to meet up with her again someday."

# Chapter 48 ~ Rectory

Father Graham was waiting patiently for Josh at the main Arrival Gate. As soon as Josh saw him, he recognized the power of the priest's countenance, the depth of his smile and the peace and compassion of his being.

"It's so good to see you again, Father, and thanks so much for coming to pick me up."

"I'm happy to do it, Josh, and look forward to continuing our discussions. I've arranged for you to stay for one week at the Guest House in Our Lady of Guadalupe Parish. It's located in the heart of downtown Palarta and has easy bus access to anywhere in the city."

"That's fantastic, Father—I can't thank you enough—and Mother and I are extremely grateful that you've agreed to preside at Cleo's, Celebration of Life."

"On the bus ride into the city, Josh and the priest got into a lively discussion."

"How would you like the Celebration for Cleo to proceed?"

"Do you have to follow any Catholic protocols?"

"No, I can do whatever I like as long as I mention the supremacy of Christ's love and his defeat of death."

"Well then," replied Josh, "I'd like it to be a quiet, respectful ceremony with time for meditation and prayer. Hopefully, there'll only be a few friends attending. I'm so glad you're not a traditionalist."

"An obituary was printed in the *Palarta Tribune* yesterday, so some people will know about it. There'll be some church congregants present who didn't even know Cleo. The actual service will take place in a small cathedral in the basement of the main church."

"That sounds just fine, Father. I'll see you soon then."

"Yes, and tomorrow afternoon I'm doing a workshop on Contemplative Prayer at the same church where you're staying. Are you interested in joining us?"

"Yes, I am Father," Josh blurted out without hesitation, "Please sign me up. What time does it start?"

"1 pm sharp in Pope Benedict's Hall—downstairs to the right of the main entrance."

Josh was dropped off at that entrance and then proceeded into the lobby of the church. A woman was waiting for him beside a bulletin board filled with colourful pamphlets and announcements.

"Josh Dunaway, I presume?"

"Yes."

"Hello sir, welcome to Our Lady's Church. My name is Sister Claire Nunez. I'm the Guest Administrator here—follow me, and I'll show you to your room."

They then walked through a side door and down a long hall before coming to a set of wide, spiral stairs.

"You're on the third floor, sir. Let's walk up to your room now."

After a long climb, they reached a series of doors. At the door with 367 on it, they stopped, and Claire bent low, placed a key in the lock and opened the door.

Josh looked in and saw a sparsely furnished but immaculately clean space. There was a single bed, a chest of drawers, a small desk and a closet. Its only window overlooked an expansive courtyard below, full of large statues of Catholic saints and popes.

"Does this room have a computer connection, Sister?"

"Yes, it does, so you're free to use your iPad at no charge. In fact, Father Graham said the cost of your whole stay here will be covered by the church."

"Wow—he's so generous."

"Yes, he's a very compassionate man. There's a communal kitchen at the end of the hall and a third-floor bathroom with communal toilets and showers two doors down."

"That's fine, Sister."

"Mass is held every morning at 7 am, followed by a light breakfast in the main kitchen. I hope to see you early tomorrow."

With that, the nun bowed and walked briskly away, leaving Josh feeling welcomed and relaxed.

# Chapter 49 ~ Heaven

As soon as Josh shut the door to his room, he sat down and opened his iPad. On it, he immediately saw Sarah's note.

*Dear Josh—*

*The baby is kicking hard now, and I think she'll be coming into this world soon. You must be here when that happens!*

*My parents are upset that you left me high and dry when we should now be on our honeymoon—but don't worry—I understand why you **had** to leave.*

*We will have to get an apartment soon because I don't want the baby growing up here. She's going to need a nursery and lots of clothes.*

*Please hurry home as soon as your business is finalized down there.*

*Love,*

*Sarah*

Josh shut his eyes in anguish after reading her words, closed his computer, and went to bed. His mind was very agitated, and it was only 6 pm. But somehow, he fell asleep and slept deeply for twelve hours. When he awoke and looked at his watch, he immediately jumped up and had a shower. After shaving and brushing his teeth, he descended into the church and reached the main cathedral by 7 am—just in time for Mass.

He was surprised to see over one hundred Mexicans in attendance. Many were lined up at the Confessional, and some were wandering around, bowing frequently.

Presently, a priest appeared in heavy, white vestments and began the service. Since the padre spoke in Spanish, Josh didn't understand a word. But he did feel a peace descending upon the congregation. He was inspired by the candles, scent of burning incense, the stain-glassed windows, and the Stations of the Cross. In particular, he was inspired by an antique painting of

Christ. Surrounded by dark tones, the body of Jesus was lit up with pure gold. Around His head was a wide halo emanating rays of pure, bright light.

Josh fell into a deep meditation as he stared at the picture. Suddenly, he felt blissful. He remembered this feeling—it came to him the last time he'd had a satori. Everything slowed down and appeared exquisitely beautiful. He stopped thinking and was very happy, fully present. It felt like his heart had opened up and was soaking in the holy atmosphere.

"This is what being in heaven must feel like," he thought.

# Chapter 50 ~ Contemplation

After the service, Josh stayed sitting in the church for over an hour. Its beauty and spiritual majesty continued to inspire him even after all the congregants had filed out and disappeared.

When he finally left the cathedral, he wandered down several cobblestoned side roads, checking out the bustling cultural idiosyncrasies of Mexico. The local people were friendly but always busy—moving this way and that through crowded, colourful street markets. Some operated the booths in those markets while others gathered around to talk, barter and smoke. Every restaurant Josh saw seemed full of boisterous, passionate patrons. He noticed that Mexicans loved to wear brightly coloured ponchos. He was surprised to see many older men holding hands with much younger women, sometimes even walking around arm in arm or stopping to kiss, or just hug—right out in the open. Some restaurants had beehives of meat turning on a stick held over an open fire.

By 1 pm, he was back at the church, anxious to get going with Father Graham's workshop on Contemplative Prayer.

Josh had no trouble finding the hall because there were signs with arrows up all over the church.

When he entered the room, he saw Father Graham presiding in a wooden chair with several people sitting in the same kind of chairs, seated around him in a circle. Josh sat down and smiled at his teacher. He had so much charisma it was awe-inspiring. The people gathered around him and listened intently to his every word.

"Welcome to this class, everyone. I want to thank you for your interest in Contemplative Prayer. My name is Father Graham, and I'm a Carmelite hermit who regularly visits all the churches in Palarta. We'll start off with five minutes of silence. Please close your eyes."

Josh fell into a deep meditation and began to feel that inner sense of peace coming back. "Would this lead to yet another satori?" He wondered.

"I want to make this session as simple as I can, folks. Please keep your eyes closed and visualize the entire Pacific Ocean. See the waves and feel the currents in this enormous body of water. Your ego—or false self—which is nothing more than the activity of thinking and feeling, will tell you that happiness lies in another part of the water. It will want you to move to that other part—but the movement *is* the problem. The waves represent your thoughts, and the currents are your feelings. Waves and currents are nothing more than agitated parts of the ocean. To find peace, real peace, you have to go down to the sea's floor. Down there, it's very still and peaceful. When you get there, you'll experience happiness. Spirituality is something you experience, not something you think about, or believe."

Josh was now calm and centred, fully present in the eternity of the moment.

"To get to the bottom of the ocean, silently repeat after me the following phrase,

***Almighty God, Thy grace is my sufficiency in all things.***

Keep going and don't stop until a feeling of joy is actually experienced. For the next ninety minutes, we'll all be completely silent."

Josh tried it. He went inside and silently repeated the phrase, over and over again. At the same time, he visualized himself sinking deeper and deeper into the ocean. Gradually, peace descended upon him—a peace which the Holy Bible had taught him, "…passeth all human understanding…". At long last, he heard the priest's calm, soft voice.

"Now you can slowly come back to the surface of the ocean and open your eyes."

All of the participants were now smiling. Some of them got up and began hugging each other.

"Don't perseverate over Catholic doctrines or beliefs, my friends—just keep doing this exercise twice a day. The session is now over," he said, "You can now go forth, taking your peace with you into the world."

Then the hermit came up to Josh and started whispering to him.

"Josh, the funeral will be held tomorrow starting at 2 pm in St. Francis Chapel on the second floor of this building. Are you willing to serve as an usher?

"Yes, sir, I am."

"Thank you. Please also beware that Alex Fernandez—Cleo's lawyer—has asked that you say a few words after the service. There'll be an open microphone."

"That's not a problem, Father; I can do that."

"Good, my son, that's very good."

Josh then walked away in a very peaceful state. Father Graham was a magical person. His very presence had calmed him down, centred his consciousness and made him relax completely.

# Chapter 51 ~ Labour

When Josh got back to his room, there was another email from Sarah waiting for him.

*Dear Josh—*

*I'm frantic! I need you here. Last night I had false labour that lasted for three hours. I thought I was going to burst wide open. My dad was just about to take me to Emergency when it subsided.*

*Can you be here on Monday? I feel so alone here right now, and my parents are not helping matters. They're constantly criticizing you.*

*Do you have any ideas on what to name our child? I'd like at least some input from you.*

*Sarah*

Josh immediately responded.

*Dear Sarah—*

*I'll be home soon—so sorry to hear about the false labour. But I'm glad you're okay now. Tell your parents to relax.*

*Yes, I do have a name picked out for our baby. How about Cleo? Perhaps her full name could be Cleo Ruby Dunaway. Your mom would like that, I'm sure.*

*Love,*

*Josh*

At that point, he sat down on his bed, pulled out his harmonica and started playing Peter Paul and Mary's song, *Leaving on a Jet Plane*, over and over again. As he played, clouds of smoke surrounded him. He felt sad but calm.

Presently, he wrote another email—this one to his mom.

*Dear Mom—*

*Cleo's service will be held tomorrow afternoon, and I've been asked to be an usher and to speak to the assembled group. It's going to be a very sad day. I think they're going to have Cleo lying in a casket at the front of the chapel.*

*I'll be thinking of you tomorrow as I know how much you loved her.*

*As always,*

*Josh*

Then he went straight to the main cathedral to pray. His intention was to use contemplative prayer to take away his chronic angst.

Later that evening, he received his mother's reply.

*Dearest Josh—*

*I'm so glad you are participating in the service tomorrow. It'll be so appropriate for you to speak about Cleo to those gathered there.*

*Please tell everyone that I loved Cleo with all my heart and will miss her terribly. If there's anything I can do at this end, let me know.*

*Love,*

*Mom oxo*

# Chapter 52 ~ Celebration

When Josh arrived at the funeral, Father Graham was already there. He was kneeling in silence at the front of the chapel. Rays of light from a nearby window shone on his face, exposing his clear complexion and calm demeanour. Before him was Cleo's open casket, strewn with flowers and bathed in coloured light, which was streaming in through a large stain-glass window. Beside the display stood a majestic, flowering cactus, which Josh recognized immediately.

She looked so dignified, graceful and serene that Josh was moved to tears. He could definitely feel her presence.

Many people filed in, and Josh led them to their places on the various hard-backed benches lined up facing the church's sanctuary. All of the people who had worked with Cleo had come to the celebration, along with over thirty devout Catholics who didn't even know her.

The priest led a solemn, sensitive, calming service punctuated by quiet organ music and muffled sighs. When Josh rose to speak, silence fell over those gathered before him.

"Cleo was an advanced soul who lived an incredibly full life here on earth. She inspired all those who met her, and she knew how to love and receive love. She had many struggles in her life and endured much suffering—but at her core was a rich vein of pure spirituality. I knew her for almost the whole of my life and stayed with her many times over the years. She was unwavering in her support of me and everything I did in life. I will treasure her and her memory forever. Cleo was a woman I loved with all my heart—and so did my mother, her best friend."

After his talk, Josh sat down mindfully. There was not a dry eye in the place—people filed by Cleo's body on their way out of the hall.

As Josh got up to leave, he was approached by a tall, handsome Mexican entirely dressed in black.

"Mr. Dunaway, my name is Alex Fernandez, and I was Cleo's lawyer. She spoke of you often and has written you a letter which she asked me to give you. Also, she wanted you to have the original copy of her will. You were, after all, her primary beneficiary. Please contact me after you've read and digested these documents."

With that, he handed Josh his business card and two large envelopes. One was labelled, *Letter to Josh*, and the other, *My Last Will and Testament.*

"And here is *my* contact information," said Josh, handing the lawyer a piece of paper.

# Chapter 53 ~ Estate

As soon as he got back to his room, Josh ripped open the letter. It was written in large, black letters on gray parchment paper.

*Dear Josh—*

*Please forgive me for doing what I did—but it was the right thing to do for me. You'll just have to believe that. After you left Mexico, I began to realize you were the love of my life, and you could never be replaced. We were a perfect match because I adored you. Your presence made me ecstatic. You are so young, so passionate, so sensitive, so masculine, and so spiritual that I just couldn't bear to live without you. I've dated three men since you left, and all were disasters. One was sensitive and caring but very effeminate. Another was strong and virile but rough and even cruel. He beat me once when he was drunk and then virtually raped me for hours. My last boyfriend was a priest, so we had a lot in common. But he wouldn't touch me. He said he loved my soul but not my body. These unsatisfying relationships were very typical for me.*

*I went to bed for the last few weeks thinking only of you, yearning for you—even though I knew you should be with Sarah, at home in Canada, raising a new family with someone your own age.*

*My work was unfulfilling, and all my friends were really only acquaintances. You were the only real kindred spirit I ever had, and I've felt so lonely these past few weeks.*

*I've decided to leave you some personal mementoes and the proceeds from the sale of my house. Perhaps that'll enable you to buy a proper home for Sarah and the baby.*

*Everything has worked out as it should. I beg you to be happy in life and remember me as an old friend from another world, another time and another generation.*

*My deepest love goes to you, for all eternity,*

*Cleo*

Josh lay down after reading it and sobbed uncontrollably. At that moment, he wished he'd stayed with Cleo in Mexico.

"This wouldn't have happened if I had," he muttered to himself.

Just then, he noticed that another email from Sarah was sitting in his "In Box."

# Chapter 54 ~ Disaster

*J*osh—

*The news is not good. I had a fight with my mother, and now she won't talk to me. Last night she left a note on my bed asking me to find another place to live. I guess she's outraged that you've disappeared. What should I do now?*

*Sarah*

Josh was horrified by the email, so he impulsively jotted a reply.

*Sarah—*

*Don't worry about where we're going to live. I do have a solution but will explain when I get home—which will be soon. Try to stay calm and focused on the baby.*

*Josh*

After sending the email, he fell into a depression. He missed Cleo terribly and didn't want to go back to Canada—at least for a long time. Feeling a need to get into the open air, he fled his confined space and ran outside into the streets of Palarta.

It was dusk, and he craved beer. Still feeling down, he went into a sleazy cantina in an alley running off one of the main thoroughfares. Sitting on a barstool, he ordered two Coors. It was dim and noisy in the cantina, so he sat still with his head hung down. A few tears dropped into his beer, and his face was red and swollen. After gulping back both drinks, he ordered another two. The friendly bartender was distracted, fat and greasy, but complied immediately.

Two hours later, Josh staggered back out into the alley. It was pitch dark by this time, and, after walking several hundred yards, he turned a corner and came onto a courtyard strewn with derelict bike and car parts. At the far end of this opening in the road, he saw four women sitting on cheap chairs in a raised enclosure, fenced in by netting. The entire porch they were sitting on was bathed in red light, coming from several red light bulbs hanging from wires protruding from a ceiling above them. One of the women was quite young—perhaps nineteen years old—but fairly attractive. She was a small Mexican woman with a colourful, red, baggy, low-cut dress covering her tanned, olive skin. Through squinted eyes, Josh noticed that she was smiling at him and motioning him to come closer.

When he reached the nylon fencing that separated this woman from him, he heard her speak.

"Come inside, Amigo; I'll move very slowly."

Without hesitating, he stepped up onto the platform and entered the porch through an opening in the awning. This brought him right next to the attractive senorita. She took his hand and said,

"Come with me."

She then tiptoed down a hallway and took Josh into a tiny, dimly lit room with bulky, yellow curtains and a double bed with red, satin sheets—but no covers. Her dress then fell to her feet, and she turned around to face him, totally naked.

Josh stared at her body and quickly saw that she was actually very appealing. Her breasts were small but curvaceous and shapely with taut brown and very erect nipples. Her waist was tiny—perhaps twelve inches around—and her prolific pubic hair was thick, bushy and jet black.

"Make love to me hard, Amigo," she whispered into his right ear before lying on the bed and spreading her legs wide apart.

As soon as his member was inserted entirely into her, Josh had a massive orgasm and filled her with every drop of stored-up semen he had. She smiled and, speaking with a raspy voice, said,

"That was good, Senor. Next time tie a knot in it. Fifty pesos, *por favor*."

Josh dressed quickly and was ushered back out onto the street. By this time, he'd sobered up a bit and realized something crazy had just happened.

"Oh my God, I didn't even use protection," he muttered to himself, "Cleo would be disgusted."

When he got back to his room, Josh found two new emails on his iPad. One was from Fernandez, and one was from Father Graham.

# Chapter 55 ~ Paydirt

Josh opened up the note from Fernandez first.

*March 20th*

*Dear Mr. Josh Dunaway,*

*Subsequent to our discussions yesterday, regarding the estate of Ms. Cleo Williams, I am writing to inform you that her home has been sold. I realize this may come as a surprise to you, as so little time has passed since her departure from this world, but such is the case.*

*A personal friend of mine has offered a price at market rates and placed a deposit in Trust. In my professional judgment, taking into account only what was in my deceased client's best interests, the appropriate course of action was to accept this offer without hesitation.*

*There is also an engraved mahogany box full of personal items for you in this estate that can be picked up once the probate on Cleo's will is fully discharged. The estimated time for completion of this process is three weeks. At that time, you'll be able to take possession of the box and a check for $329,425 in Canadian funds, which is the total amount paid for Cleo's home, less closing costs. Should you wish to have these items mailed to you, please inform me of such as soon as possible.*

*Sincerely,*

*Alex Fernandez*

*Curillo & Associates*

*Palarta*

Josh was so stunned and confused by the contents of this message that he didn't know what to think. So he didn't think about it. Instead, he quickly opened the email from his mentor.

*Dear Josh—*

*Thank you for speaking at Cleo's service yesterday. I feel we gave her a worthy send-off. Hopefully, you're now reaping the profound rewards of contemplative prayer.*

*Tomorrow I'll be heading back to the hermitage for some intense prayer and fasting. However, I'll only be away for two weeks as I'll participate in some of the Lenten Series Celebrations at this church during Easter.*

*If you'd like to accompany me to the monastery for these two weeks, please let me know by 9 pm tonight. Perhaps you could consider this an opportunity for a much-needed Retreat to gain some clarity in your life. I hope you'll consider this break dependent, of course, on your ability to reschedule your flight back to Canada.*

*In Peace,*

*Father Graham*

Josh knew he had to go into a deep meditation before responding to Father Graham's communication. But before he did that, he knocked off a brief reply to Fernandez.

*Mr. Fernandez—*

*Thank you for your letter and your legal work regarding the file of Cleo Williams. I now understand all of my options. I would like to inform you that I'd like to have both the mahogany box and a certified check sent to my home address when the probate process is complete.*

*Please send these items to my best friend's house. His address is—*

*Bruce McRae, 1812 Oak Street, Valleytown, BC  V95 4Y7*

*Josh Dunaway*

# Chapter 56 ~ Pause

Later that day, Josh knocked on the door of the padre's room. When he appeared in front of him, Josh said,

"Father Graham, I've been able to delay my flight home for two weeks and would like to join you on the coast for prayer, fasting and a bit of guidance."

"That's wonderful, my son. I'm very happy about that. Please meet me on St. Jerome Street behind the church at 5 am tomorrow morning. I'll be driving a red Volkswagen."

"Can I bring my cigarettes, Father?"

"No, that wouldn't be appropriate."

Josh then went back to his room to pack and prepare for the trip. After supper, he wrote two emails—one to his mother and one to Sarah.

*Dear Mom—*

*Cleo's funeral went well, as far as funerals go. I felt her presence in the chapel and mentioned in my talk how much both of us loved her. People said my words touched them.*

*My flight home has been delayed for two weeks. I'll now be arriving in Valley-town on April 7th. I'm thinking of you and trust that all is well.*

*Love,*

*Josh*

He then continued working on his computer by composing a note to Sarah.

*Dear Sarah—*

*Cleo's service went well beyond the intense grief that struck me and continues to tear away at my heart. I spoke at her service, and later met with her lawyer.*

*I'm worried about you and the baby, but know that soon all our troubles will be over. Cleo left me some money. Her home was bequeathed to me, and it's already sold for well over 300 k in Canadian funds.*

*You can start looking for a townhouse because I'll be able to buy us our own place in about a month.*

*I'll be home in just over two weeks, arriving in Valleytown on April 7th. Sorry to be taking so long, but I've got an opportunity to study at Father Graham's monastery and really need this time to deal with my depression. It's not a serious problem or anything—it's just that I feel overwhelmed with many things happening in my life right now.*

*I won't be able to contact or speak to you in any way until I get home. Please pick me up at the airport at 9:37 pm on April 7th at the International Terminal. I'll be on Flight 67295.*

*Love,*

*Josh*

Just before he packed up his mouth organ, and just before he went to bed, Josh played the full rendition of Dylan's *Mr. Tambourine Man* over and over again. After puffing away a full smoke, he set his alarm and fell into a deep sleep.

# Chapter 57 - Paradise

Josh was waiting at the priest's car when he arrived.

"Thanks for being so punctual, Josh," he said.

With that, he placed Josh's backpack into the vehicle's trunk and opened the passenger door for him to get seated. Josh noticed how slowly he moved, as if in slow motion. Every step he took was measured and conscious. Just sitting beside him made Josh feel calm and relaxed. Father Graham's presence was powerful because he was a man overflowing with compassion, and that compassion spilled over and embraced anyone receptive to it.

The trip to the coast was very pleasant. Once they got outside the city limits, there was virtually no traffic, and the scenery was breathtaking. At first, they passed through groves of palm trees, then the landscape became more sparse with scrub brush and cacti bordering the dusty, unpaved road.

It was dawn. A bright yellow sun slowly peered over the distant hills and began to bathe the entire desert in warmth and light. The countryside was waking up, coming to life after a long night's sleep.

"Have you been able to work on the solitary confinement exercise, Josh, and calm your demons down?"

"Yes, I have Father—and it *has* helped. But sometimes, I get into situations that are overwhelming for me. When that happens, I get triggered, and a particular demon shows up and bites me. That demon is sexual and makes me behave self-destructively. I get overcome by lust."

"Don't worry, Josh—you *are* making progress. For now, try to avoid those situations until your inner development grows more stable. Remember, the demons are not entities. They're projections of pain and trauma you've endured in your life and then suppressed—creating heavy, black thoughts attached to feelings. Those feelings and thoughts **are** the demons. Be compassionate with yourself, and you'll transform your inner pain and lust into bliss. But it takes time. The peace you're seeking lies within you, *underneath* your suffering. You have to go straight through that suffering, and not avoid it, to find the peace."

"Thanks, Father, you're an inspiration to me. Sometimes your teachings don't seem to follow Catholic theology, but your actions are always pure and clean. You seem to be continually living in the present moment."

After three hours on a dusty, dirt road, they passed a village called Esoterica. On the other side of that very small town stood a sign that read *Monastery of Carmel—2 km*. A few minutes later, they reached the hermitage. As they drove into the enclave, Josh saw a sign reading, *The Mexican Monastery of Carmel*. Then he noticed a small chapel sitting alongside a wooden, fenced-in building with a peaked roof. Inside that building were three sets of bunk beds in a large room with a small kitchen at one end. There was no electricity, so the kitchen stove burned wood—a simple well piped in water to an enamel sink with many chips in it. There was only one tap.

"You can sleep on any one of these beds, Josh. My abode is a small hut on the other side of that sand dune. Now, let me show you the chapel."

The church was very compact but well-constructed and sun-baked on the outside. At its front end, inside stood a beautiful altar with a heavy, oak communion table behind it and a cream-coloured tablecloth draped over it. A life-sized replica of Michelangelo's *Pieta*, showing Jesus in Mary's arms, stood beside it—roped off from public access.

Walking outside and around the building, Josh could hear crashing surf—they were only fifty feet away from the beach! And it was a pristine and solitary beach with turquoise water, bubbling surf and pure white sand—stretching for miles down the coast.

"This is paradise," thought Josh. "In this place, I'll be able to get lots of work done on my novel and sort out my whole life."

"Prayer will begin in the chapel tomorrow morning at 4 am, Josh," said Father Graham. Then I'll impose monastic rules which will put us into a healing routine."

"I'll see you in the morning, then, Father Graham," replied Josh.

# Chapter 58 ~ Discipline

Father Graham prodded Josh at exactly 3:30 am and caused him to jump out of bed. "Let's go to chapel now, young man," he whispered.

Josh immediately pulled on his gray track pants, a bulky sweater and the sandals Sarah had given him for the trip. He went directly to the front of the church; he knelt down while the padre stood very erect at the lectern. He was smiling and seemed very happy.

"Our reading today is from Isaiah 43:1,7,10.11; and 44: 6—8."

> *I am the first, and I am the last, and beside me, there is no God. And who, as I, shall call, and shall declare it, and set it in order for me, since I appointed the ancient people? And the things that are coming, and shall come, let them show unto them. Fear ye not, neither be afraid: have not I told thee from that time, and have declared it? Ye are even my witnesses. Is there a God beside me? Yes, there is no God; I know not any.*

"Now, let us pray."

With that, the Father sat down on a bench beside Josh's seat and closed his eyes, moving his right hand up and across his body three times, with the sign of the cross.

"Let's move into contemplative prayer, Josh."

Josh closed his eyes and visualized himself bobbing on the Pacific Ocean. Then he saw himself sinking down, down, down…to the very bottom of the sea. It was still down there and very quiet. His thoughts began to slow down noticeably.

He stayed in that silence for over an hour—until he heard a bell-like sound. It was Father striking a chime with a padded stick.

"I'm so calm and peaceful now."

"That's good, Josh. You are now fully present and collected. How does that make you feel?"

"Like everything is perfect and sacred exactly the way it is."

"Good work, my son. Here is our daily schedule, "as he passed Josh a sheet of paper. It read—

| | |
|---|---|
| **3:30 am** | **RISE** |
| **3:45** | **READING** |
| **3:50** | **CONTEMPLATIVE PRAYER** |
| **5:00** | **MASS** |
| **6:00** | **CHANTING** |
| **7:00** | **BREAKFAST** |
| **8:00** | **WORK** |
| **12:00** | **EXAMINATION OF CONSCIENCE** |
| **1:30** | **DINNER** |
| **2:00** | **FREE TIME** |
| **4:00** | **TEA BREAK** |
| **4:30** | **CONTEMPLATIVE PRAYER** |
| **5:30** | **SUPPER** |
| **6:30** | **FREE TIME** |
| **8:00** | **EXAMINATION OF CONSCIENCE** |
| **9:00** | **SOLITUDE IN SILENCE** |
| **10:00** | **RETIRE** |

Thus began Josh's first monastic experiences. They were difficult at first, but he began to adjust to the intense and disciplined routines after three days. Father Graham performed a full Mass every day, including breaking bread and the celebration of Holy Communion. This was followed by a full hour of chanting. Meals were simple but nutritious—and included fresh vegetables, fruit, monastic bread, water and canned meat. Josh was assigned yard duties during the work periods, which included pulling weeds in the garden, picking fruit, and clearing bushes. When it came to Free Time, Josh found he was able to write profusely. At last, he seemed to contact his creative side. Pages and pages of writing flowed out of him daily—and he knew it was good stuff.

However, it was the periods of *Examination of Conscience* that proved most spiritually valuable to Josh. On his first day of monastic life, he confessed a major sin to his spiritual guide.

# Chapter 59 ~ Confession

At exactly twelve noon on that first day, the Father said, "Josh, please go behind that black curtain at the side of the church, sit in the chair, and get ready for an **Examination of Conscience**."

"Yes, Father."

Once behind the veil, Father Graham asked, "Are there any sins you want to confess, my son?"

"Yes, there is one—and it's a big one."

"What is it?"

"Holy Father, two days ago, I had unprotected sex with a Mexican prostitute. Can you possibly forgive me? I was depressed and drunk and became vulnerable to a demon within me that took over my whole consciousness. Now I'm full of guilt and remorse. It feels like I'm in a downward spiral right now."

"That demon was a black hole of suppressed pain, and it *was* powerful, but it could **never** take over your whole consciousness because your whole consciousness is the infinity of God. Please repeat after me the following words. Say them slowly, meditatively.

**Mary, Mother of God, have mercy on my soul and forgive my many sins."**

He began repeating the petition and kept repeating it until the padre stopped speaking it—after about fifteen minutes.

"Josh, you're forgiven. Tomorrow you must start fasting. The fast will last for two days and culminate with a *laying on of hands* ceremony. Then, next week, before you leave the monastery, we'll do a cactus connection exercise. This will make sure the purification of your soul is complete."

"What is a cactus connection?"

"You'll soon know, my son. Now it's time to work in the yard. The temperature is currently 110 degrees F. The heat and labour will help cleanse your soul."

After clearing brush with a very heavy sickle for three hours, Josh collapsed onto the sand. Father Graham picked him up, carried him into the bunkhouse and splashed a pail of cold water over his face. As he came to, Josh felt currents of energy rushing through his whole body.

"I feel so clean, so calm, so happy, Father. What happened to me? The last thing I remember was working next to you in the desert."

"You're going through a process of spiritual healing, Josh. Once completely free of your inner pain, you'll be able to live fully in the present moment, and your consciousness will have a healing effect on others."

"Is the laying on of hands a part of this healing?"

"Yes."

"How about the cactus connection?"

"Yes."

"I can't wait," replied Josh as his eyes lit up with joy.

# Chapter 60 ~ Freedom

The next two days were extremely difficult. But despite the physical suffering Josh endured, his spiritual faculties seemed to heighten.

It was hot, very hot. He felt that heat as an oppressive element as he slipped into total silence. As the two days passed, his hunger mounted—but it also made everything in his inner life sharpen, coming into a clear focus. Could his intense suffering be transformed into joy?

On the second day of his fast, the Father said,

"Come with me to the beach now."

When they got to the water's edge, Josh heard the crashing of the surf and saw that the priest had set a fire in the barbeque pit. They sat down on logs beside the pit.

"Let's close our eyes and pray," said Father Graham.

*"This battle is not yours, but God's. Be strong and courageous. The world is only an arm of flesh; with you is the Lord God, to help you and to fight your battles."*

With that, he lit the fire. Slowly, the wood began to crackle and throw light into the darkness of the night. Once the fire was raging, Father told Josh to take off his shirt. Then he placed his hands on Josh's shoulders, squeezing tightly.

*"By the power vested in me through the agency of the Holy Spirit, I command you, lustful demon, to flee—NOW."*

Then he looked to the heavens and screamed, "Heal Josh, heal. Now you're free."

Josh's body tightened and shook all over as he started a series of dry heaves. Then he fell to the ground and felt the flames burning his starved body. Suddenly, he felt like he'd just vomited a bad meal that had been poisoning him. His entire being was bathed in compassion, peace—and love for everything in the universe. His compulsive thoughts had stopped. Inside he was silent, clean, and fully present.

"I'm free, Father Graham, I'm free."

"Yes," replied the hermit, "Freedom is experiencing God directly and surrendering to him totally."

"Now you're ready for the cactus connection, Josh."

"Yes I am, Father, yes I am."

# Chapter 61 ~ The Power of a Flowering Cactus

For the rest of his stay, Josh soaked up the Carmelite disciplines with enthusiasm. It felt like he was making real spiritual progress. Most importantly, he was writing copious amounts of words on a daily basis. He'd once read a great definition of the word 'writer'. "A writer," it said, "is a person who writes." Now he felt he could legitimately call himself a writer.

On the day scheduled for his cactus exercise, Josh had an interesting conversation with his guru.

"Father, when you did the laying on of hands last week, you called out my sexual demon as though it were a real malevolent being. Yet you've taught me such vampires have no reality. I'm confused."

Let me explain it this way, Josh. Imagine you have a dream, and you dream about a demon chasing you. In your dream, that creature is real—it's chasing you and causing you to experience fear or even terror. But when you wake up out of the dream, you realize nothing really happened. The demon was real only in the dream. In reality, you were lying asleep, safe in your bed, all night long. That's the way it is with demons. Ultimately, nothing exists but God. It's just a matter of *experiencing* the reality of this truth.

Later that afternoon, they headed over a sand dune about half a kilometre from the chapel. Now it was time to conduct the cactus connection. After walking over a ridge, Josh saw a giant cactus—perhaps fifteen feet high. It was glistening in the sunlight and was covered with hundreds of crimson flowers—in full bloom.

"Look at that plant, Josh. Stare at it. This is an important being, and it **is** real, and it can teach you a great deal. This is not a dream. This cactus lives here alone in the parched, desolation of the desert and yet somehow manages to thrive. Its roots travel long distances to find moisture, and then they haul that wetness home. Its prickles protect it from any enemies that might try to dislocate its peace. And it not only survives, but it also flourishes and produces beautiful flowers and scents. You can learn to be like this cactus when you get back to civilization. Do you see the miracle in all of this?"

"Yes, Father, I do."

"Good, now kneel beside the plant and close your eyes. Imagine that this cactus has veins just like yours. Do you see them?"

"Yes."

"Now—visualize a series of hoses joining your veins to the veins of the cactus. Are you feeling connected to it?"

"Yes."

"Now, imagine that a healing juice is circulating between you and the plant. Imagine you're joined to the plant—that you **are** the cactus. Can you feel the juices running through your body?"

"Yes."

"Stay there. Stay kneeling. Feel the juices entering your being—cleaning and healing you."

Josh felt waves of energy shooting into him, flowing through him and cleaning him out. It was overwhelming. After thirty minutes of this visualization exercise, he fell to the sand and passed out.

When he woke up, Father Graham was standing over him, pointing a crucifix toward his chest. It felt like his heart was literally opening, like a bud in the springtime responding to the sun's radiant warmth.

"Bless you, Josh. How do you feel now?"

"I feel ecstatic, Father. I've never felt so happy."

He sat up and let the sun's rays penetrate his soul. He stayed in a state of utter bliss for over two hours while Father Graham prayed. On their way back to the bunkhouse, the priest said,

"You'll feel connected to every cactus you see now—for the rest of your life."

# Chapter 62 ~ Civilization

On the drive back to Palarta, Josh was wholly composed as he dialogued with the monk. "Some important shifts have taken place in me, Father."

"How do you mean?"

"It feels like a space of tranquillity has opened up in my head. That space is absorbing all my problems."

"That's wonderful, Josh."

"Also, my craving for cigarettes has fallen away. I've smoked for ten years, and now I have no desire to touch tobacco."

"That's what happens to addictions when you experience spiritual healing, son."

As they drove along through the desert, heading to the coast, Josh felt extremely sensitive to the beauty of the natural world they were passing. Plants, shrubs, palm trees, tumbleweeds and particularly cacti appeared sacred and throbbing with life.

"I now feel deeply connected to nature. In the past, I didn't notice how alive the desert is. Why is that?"

"You've tapped into every living thing because all your energy blocks were lowered at Carmel. However, stay vigilant—they can rise up again if you go unconscious."

As they approached the city and traffic became dense, Josh realized how toxic modern civilization had become. At the airport, he checked in while Father Graham held his flight bag. When it came time to head to the departure gate, he felt very emotional.

"I'm going to miss you so much, Father," he said as tears welled up.

"Don't worry, we'll be in touch."

"Can you give me any final advice?"

"Yes. The spiritual life is very simple. Stop throughout the day to meditate. Close your eyes, and let go of everything. Fall back into God. **He will guide you.**"

"What about the solitary confinement exercise?"

"Continue to isolate yourself and embrace your demons with compassion and non-judgment. Be patient. They can become your allies if you stay present to them and their wants—-without flinching."

"You inspire me, Father."

"Thank you and good-bye, Josh. Trust me—you *are* making progress."

As Josh climbed into his seat in preparation for take-off, his mind turned to Sarah.

"I hope she's waiting for me when we land," he thought.

# Chapter 63 ~ Birth

Josh left the plane quickly once it landed and stopped at the Valleytown International Airport. As soon as he entered the Arrivals Lounge, he was shocked to see his good friend Bruce standing there, waiting for him.

"Great to see you, bud," he called out.

"Yes, it is, Bruce, but where's my wife?"

"She's in the Maternity Ward at Valleytown Memorial. You're now the father of a very healthy daughter."

Oh, my God," he replied, "I missed the whole birth. Can you take me to the hospital now?"

"Yeah, sure, let's go."

On the way to visit Sarah, Josh and his friend had an important conversation which helped prepare the new father for what was to come.

"I want to warn you, my friend, Sarah's not a happy camper. She can't believe you weren't there for the baby's arrival. And don't forget, the baby was three weeks overdue—that makes your late arrival hurt even more."

"Three weeks late? She was never clear on the due date. Oh my God…Do you think she'll understand my predicament when I tell her I was experiencing incredible healings at a spiritual retreat?"

"No—it won't mean a thing to her."

Once he got to the door of his wife's room, he asked Bruce to sit in the hall and wait. When he finally saw Sarah, she was subdued. Her face was red, puffy and tear-stained.

"Hi, Sarah, so good to see you."

"Josh, I'm really pissed off. When the baby came, your friend Bruce was the only one in the delivery room with me, and I had to have a Caesarian birth. You were four thousand miles away at the time."

"That's totally unacceptable," Josh answered in loud tones. "Where was your Mom?"

"She isn't talking to me right now, and my parents want us out of their house by the end of April."

"Why would you ask a friend of mine to be with you at such an intimate time?"

"Because he was the only one around who cared."

"Look, I got delayed by an intense spiritual retreat that was very good for me and good for us."

"How could that be good for me?"

"Because I got rid of a lot of my baggage and can now focus better on our relationship."

At that point, a nurse arrived at Sarah's bed—pushing a cart. Inside it, under a pink blanket, was a very beautiful baby girl. She had huge blue eyes and wisps of curly red hair just above her exquisitely formed ears.

"Meet your daughter, Josh. Her name is Cleo Ruby Dunaway."

# Chapter 64 ~ Friends

On the way home from the hospital, Josh asked his friend, "Can we go for a beer? We have to talk."

"Okay, sure."

Once they were seated, Josh ordered four drinks. A hurried waitress dropped four glasses of Golden Murphy Ale onto their small round table. Before he started to speak, Josh sloshed down a whole beer.

"Did you find some peace down there in Mexico?" Bruce asked.

"Absolutely, I did. It was amazing. I had this incredible teacher who took me to profound places. We did some powerful exercises, and I was able to drop a lot of the poison that was inside me—and find some peace of mind, body and soul."

"I don't believe in any of that religious crap, but it sounds like you had a great time."

"Yeah, and I came away feeling this sense of tranquillity and acceptance of life *as it is*. Unfortunately, ever since I got back to Canada, some of that peace seems to be draining away."

"Don't worry, my friend. Things will settle down now that you're home. Did you get any work done on your novel?"

"Yes, I did. When I was at the retreat, the writing flowed from me. I've got fifteen chapters written and know where the story's going. Some of my characters are taking on a life of their own."

"That's fabulous—keep it up."

"Yes, I definitely will. But now I have to go back to driving a hack. It'll be a long time before I can make money with my writing."

"Did they hold your taxi job for you?"

"That'll be no problem—they're always desperate for drivers. How's your work going?"

"Just great—I've been hired on at Point Cape Shipyards doing marine mechanical work. They're desperate for anyone with mechanical training who is willing to work tons of overtime. The money is outrageous."

"Wow," exclaimed Josh as he bent forward and looked right into his friend's eyes. Bruce, this is a crazy request, but I'm going to make it anyway. Is there any way Sarah and I and the baby could stay with you for about three weeks? Her parents are furious with us. There's no way I can go back there to live."

"Will Sarah be okay with that idea?"

"I don't think she has many choices. Besides, Cleo's house sold, and I'm going to be coming into some money from that sale."

"How much?"

"Over 300 k."

"Bloody hell."

"So, we're going to buy a small townhouse right away. We'll be out of your place in a month, trust me."

"Josh, you're my best friend. If you need a place to stay, my flat is yours. When do you want to move in?"

"Tomorrow."

That night, Josh quickly dashed off a note to his mother.

*Dear Mom—*

*I arrived safely yesterday, and Bruce picked me up at the airport. Sarah wasn't able to come out to get me because she was in the hospital—recovering after the delivery of our beautiful, healthy baby girl. We're naming her Cleo Ruby Dunaway.*

*We'll be moving into Bruce's place soon as Sarah has some issues with her parents right now.*

*All is well. Hope you can get down to see the baby very soon.*

*Love, Josh*

He was tempted to have a cigarette before hitting the sack. Instead, he picked up his harmonica and played a few bars of Glenn Campbell's *Rhinestone Cowboy*. That put him into a state where sleep was easy.

# Chapter 65 ~ Bonding

The next day, after arranging to return to his job and working his first shift, Josh was back in the hospital, visiting his wife and baby. Sarah was lying in bed with baby Cleo propped up beside her.

"Did you get my email about the inheritance from Cleo Williams?"

"Yes, and that *is* good news. But aren't you going to give your baby a kiss?"

Hearing that, Josh bent low and gave the tiny child a peck on the cheek.

"She's a doll, Sarah. Have you been looking for a place to live?"

"Yes, and I've found one."

"What's it like?"

"It's a gorgeous condominium near Playfair Mall. The ceilings are vaulted and angled and reach a height of twenty-one feet at their peak. It's got two large bedrooms, hardwood floors, granite countertops and four brand new appliances."

"Wow, you've done your homework. I can't wait to see it. How much is it?"

"Only 297 k."

"We can pay cash for it then—and get started on a life together."

"Yes."

"In the meantime," Josh relayed, "We're going to have to live with Bruce. He's got a spare bedroom we can use, and he won't charge us any rent. All we have to do is buy our own food."

"Now there's a true friend. You always know who your real friends are at any time a crisis occurs. I'm getting out of here tomorrow, Josh. Maybe you could look at the condo I want once we move into Bruce's place?"

"That'll work. What time shall I pick you up?"

"After lunch, say about 1 pm."

"Okay, and how are we going to get all our stuff?"

"I moved everything into Sally's basement after Mom, and I had that big fight."

"Who's Sally?"

"A friend I went to school with who happens to live in a mansion with tons of extra space."

"It's a good thing we don't own too much stuff. And why are you crying?"

"Don't you want to pick up your daughter?" she stammered, tears streaming down her face.

Josh picked up Cleo, walked around the room with her briefly, and then put her back down on Sarah's pillow.

"Aren't you feeling bonded to her?"

"Yes, I think I'm starting to, Sarah. She *is* beautiful. I'll see you tomorrow after lunch."

"Bye, Josh."

# Chapter 66 ~ Suspicions

They moved into Bruce's apartment on April 30th with little fanfare. Almost everything they owned was squeezed into the spare bedroom. Since there were two single beds, sleeping was going to be cramped. Cleo was placed in a basket on the floor.

That afternoon, Sarah showed her husband the condo she had her heart set on.

"Look at how high the ceilings are, Josh, and the pine floors. This place is immaculate. Do you like the designer kitchen?"

"Doesn't it bother you that it's on a really busy street?" asked Josh.

"We'll get used to it in time. I never listen to traffic anyway. Now come and have a look at the nursery."

"The second bedroom is nice, Sarah, but this place is small and noisy. It's not a great space to meditate or write."

"Maybe you could go to a church to meditate and a library to write?"

"Sarah, this is not my kind of place. But if you want it, I'll make an offer on it."

"You will?"

"Yes."

"I love you for that, Darling," she whispered as she put her arm around his waist and pulled him close.

Josh was able to purchase the property for 285 k and budget 15 k for new furniture. After borrowing $500 from Bruce, he was able to put $1000 down and secure the property by informing the realtor that he'd have the rest of the money—in cash—by closing time at month's end. They were scheduled to move in on June 1, and Sarah was overjoyed.

The next day a package arrived at Bruce's apartment addressed to Josh from a Mexican legal firm. As soon as he saw it, he knew what the box contained. After quickly ripping its brown packaging off, he found a certified check for $387,000 Canadian dollars and three small objects. The first was a hand-carved wooden crucifix with a leather strap attached so he could wear it around his neck. The second was a beautiful jade statue of St. Francis of Assisi. Underneath those items was a thick book full of interesting illustrations. Its title was *Finding Nirvana Through Sex*, by Cleo Williams.

"Cleo was the best friend I ever had," he thought, after opening his gifts. "and she wrote a book I can't wait to read."

Living in his friend's place was barely tolerable. Bruce's apartment was small that there was hardly any room for privacy. Sex was totally out of the question, although Sarah had hinted that she'd be ready to make love to Josh when they moved.

"My stitches should be completely healed by then," she had said.

Bruce was a friendly host, but strangely, Josh sometimes felt he was *too* friendly with his wife. One day he came in quietly and, when he peeked into his bedroom, saw Sarah changing the baby's diaper while Bruce rubbed her back.

"That's not appropriate," he thought. He also thought it was strange that Bruce paid so much attention to Cleo.

Sitting on Bruce's fluffy couch just before moving day, Josh felt queasy about their living arrangement. That was just before Sarah came up to him and put the baby in his lap, and said,

"Don't you love her dimple?"

"Oh my God," he pondered, "That's exactly the same dimple—in exactly the same spot—as the one on Bruce's chin."

As distracted as he was, he noticed a note from his mother as he walked by his computer. It read—

*Dear Josh—*

*I'm overjoyed that you're the proud father of a healthy girl. Cleo would be delighted that you named the baby after her! I'll be able to see her soon as I've got two weeks of vacation time left in June. You're one lucky man!*

*Hug Sarah and Cleo for me. Love y'all.*

*Mom*

# Chapter 67 ~ Confrontation

After supper the next day, Josh said, "Bruce, let's go for a beer. We've got to talk."

"Sure, bud', what's up?"

"I'll tell you when we get to the pub."

At the bar, they both ordered beers and sat at a square table in the corner. It was secluded and quiet there, and the area was dimly lit.

"You seem to be getting close to Sarah, my friend."

"How do you mean?"

"You two get along really well. And you're also developing a real bond with Cleo."

"They're great people, Josh."

"Bruce, tell me the absolute truth. Have you ever screwed my wife?"

"Why in the hell would you even *think* that?" replied Bruce, turning beat red.

"Because the baby looks exactly like you."

A heavy silence descended upon the table before Bruce whispered,

"It only happened once, Josh, I swear. I swear on a stack of bibles. I'm sorry."

"When did it happen?"

"Three weeks after you left for Mexico the first time, Sarah came by my place to drop off a book you'd left at her place."

"Then what happened?"

"She told me she was sweaty from running and asked if she could have a shower. I said, sure—of course. After her shower, she came into my kitchen wrapped in a skimpy towel, all wet and dripping all over the floor."

"What did she do next?"

"Dropped the towel and stood there stark naked, smiling at me. I was going to turn and walk away but couldn't take my eyes off her breasts. They're huge. She put both my hands on them and asked me to massage her."

"*Where* did you screw her?"

"On top of the kitchen counter. Everything happened so fast—honestly, it was over in five minutes. I regret it all now but don't forget—you two had broken up. I told her I didn't feel right about being her boyfriend. Nothing else happened after that."

"Bruce, you're Cleo's father, I know it."

"How do you know?"

"Call it intuition. Will you do a paternity test so we can know for sure?"

"Why?"

"Before I discuss this with Sarah, I have to know who the baby's father is."

"Can you forgive me for doing this, Josh?"

"Yes."

# Chapter 68 ~ Tests

Over the next week, two critical medical tests were undertaken. Josh went to an STD Clinic, and Bruce attended Valleytown Memorial for a paternity test. A few days later, they both received official letters.

Josh's read,

> *Dear Sir,*
>
> *Please be advised that your recent Sweeping STD and AIDS Specific tests have been completed.*
>
> *Your results were on all counts were*
>
> *Negative    x*
>
> *Positive*
>
> *This means you have been given a clean bill of health.*
>
> *Joan Dawson*
>
> *Medical Adjudicator*
>
> *Western STD Clinic*

The other stated,

> *Mr. McRae,*
>
> *Our hospital lab has compared blood samples from the recently born Cleo Ruby Dunaway and yourself.*
>
> *Results show a 99% probability that you are this baby's father.*
>
> *Should you require more detailed information, please contact Mary Schneider. Her contact information is enclosed under a separate cover.*
>
> *Sincerely,*

*Paul Morgan*

*Lab Sciences Unit 12*

*Valleytown Memorial Hospital*

After reading the document, Bruce called his friend. "The results are in, and you were right—I'm her father."

"I knew it," spluttered Josh. "Thanks for getting it done. I'll talk to you later."

When he came home from work that day, he told Sarah, "We're going out for supper tonight."

"Alright, what's the occasion?"

"I'm just in the mood to celebrate."

They went to a fancy French diner, and Josh ordered an expensive bottle of Merlot before dinner. He slowly poured red wine into his wife's glass.

"Are you excited about moving into our place, Josh?"

"Sarah, I'm not moving into our condo?"

"Pardon me?"

"It's not going to work for me, but I want you to move there."

"For God's sake, why would you do this?"

"First of all, I can't stand the place. I'm a writer and need lots of quiet time and space. Secondly, I'm not Cleo's father and feel we got married under false pretenses."

"What do you mean you're not her father—of course, you are!"

"Did you not notice Cleo's red, curly hair and the dimple on her chin? Those are the exact same features Bruce has.

"That just couldn't be, Josh."

Bruce just had a paternity test that proves it, Sarah. You had sex with him once and got pregnant."

"Josh, please…listen to me—it was an accident and should never have happened. I'm sorry, but you and I weren't together then."

"I forgive you for having sex with my best friend. But I'll never understand why you called me back from Mexico for this."

Sarah didn't respond. She just sat in her chair silently, embarrassed and shocked.

"I had no idea Bruce was the father, Josh. I'm not perfect, you know."

"Look, I'm not perfect either," Josh went on.

"What does that mean?"

"I got drunk and had unprotected sex with a hooker in Mexico. But don't worry, I've been tested, and I'm clean."

"What about our marriage?"

"I'll be filing for divorce."

Sarah was crying hysterically by then and stood up just as her plate of spaghetti and meatballs arrived. Then she quickly left the table and ran out of the restaurant into the darkness of the night.

# Chapter 69 ~ Motel

The next day, Josh moved into the Shoreline Motel. It was an establishment situated right on the edge of the Shoreline River. It allowed forty percent of its space to be occupied by permanent residents. His suite was small but adequate to fulfill his needs. It had a bed, a desk, a closet, a full bathroom and a small kitchenette with a fridge, sink, microwave and a tiny table. Rent was $1200—a sum he could now handily afford. As soon as he settled in, he wrote two email notes. The first was to his mother.

*Dear Mom—*

*I hate to disappoint you, but I do have shocking news! Despite the emotional happiness I've felt about becoming a parent, it turns out the biological father is my best friend, Bruce*

*At this time, Sarah and I have decided to separate again, and it's not entirely due to the mix-up involving Cleo.*

*The truth of the matter is we are not compatible. Sarah is a beautiful woman with great promise as a wife to someone and a mother to Cleo—but we're simply not on the same wavelength.*

*I don't know what the future holds except that I want to be a writer, and that's a career Sarah cannot fully support.*

*Shortly, she'll be moving with the baby into a condo that we recently bought. Right now, I'm staying at a motel in town. My intention is to maintain positive and meaningful relationships with Sarah, Cleo and Bruce in the weeks, months and years ahead.*

*More details later.*

*Josh.*

The second was to Sarah. It read,

*Dear Sarah—*

*I'm sorry I was so confrontative with you the last time we were together. But you have to admit some pretty disturbing matters came up.*

*I've got great admiration and respect for you and hold nothing against you for anything that has happened between us during the entire span of our relationship.*

*After contemplating the matter deeply, I realize that, at this time, a legal divorce petition is not necessary. If this should change in the future, and either one of us ever desires to remarry, we can deal with it then. But I **am** clear that our married life is over. The reason? We're simply not travelling down the same paths in life.*

*I've decided to give you the condominium, as I want you and Cleo to get off to a good start and have some stability in your lives. I'll transfer the title to your name alone and arrange for you to see my lawyer sign the appropriate documents when they're ready.*

*My sincere hope is that we'll remain friends forever.*

*Josh*

After he'd finished those notes, he sat down on his bed and played Paul McCartney's signature song, *Yesterday*, over and over again. Then he pulled Celeste's business card out of his wallet and phoned her—leaving a message on her answering machine.

*"Hi, Celeste—I hope you remember me from the flight we took to Mexico a few months ago. I'd like to book a massage with you as soon as possible. My email address is joshinow@turf.com."*

# PART 3 – CELESTE

# Chapter 70 - Equilibrium

Josh began to regain some inner peace and tranquillity after he established himself in the motel. It had become apparent that the recent turmoil in his life had knocked him off track as far as his spiritual progress was concerned.

He started running again. Running the way Cleo had taught him—counting his breaths until he could let go and move effortlessly, no matter how fast his legs were moving.

He resumed his solitary confinement exercises with a particular focus on embracing and transforming his sexual demon. He also practiced the Pacific Ocean contemplative prayer process given to him by his teacher. That meant he was spending up to ninety minutes a day in deep contemplations—even though he was still working full time as a cab driver.

He also bought a flowering cactus two feet tall. He replanted it into a huge ceramic container full of mushroom-enhanced soil. That cactus sat prominently beside a window near his bed. It was a plant that Josh began to feel intimately connected to. Sometimes he found himself talking to it. Whenever the cactus was thirsty, he watered it immediately. It was a magical plant.

Not long after he'd started to regain his composure, a strong urge to communicate with Father Graham arose within him. His text read—

*Dear Father—*

*I pray you are well and keeping happy.*

*As for me, I've just come through some very disturbing times. You might even say it was a period of darkness, perhaps like St. John's 'dark night of the soul.'*

*Sarah and I broke up for good after it became evident that her baby had been biologically fathered by my best friend. I ended the relationship and gave her a condo I'd bought for us. That still left me with a bit of a nest egg to start life anew.*

*At the moment, I'm living in a motel—which has created a very simple lifestyle— but the place has all the amenities I need to keep moving forward.*

*I've been able to resume my prayers and meditations and continue to listen for guidance and inspiration from the Holy Spirit.*

*On top of all of this, I've started writing again and am making excellent progress with my novel.*

*More on that later,*

*In Peace,*

*Josh.*

As soon as he completed this communication, he noticed an incoming note from Celeste. It read—

*Josh—*

*So good to hear from you, and yes—I do remember well our time on that flight to Mexico.*

*I can schedule you for a full body massage next Tuesday from 9:30 am – 11. Will that work for you?*

*Ciao,*

*Celeste*

Josh immediately responded with a text of his own.

*Celeste—*

*Thanks for responding to my text. I look forward to talking to you again. I'll see you next week for a massage.*

*Cheers!*

*Josh*

He then sat on his bed, gazed at his cactus, and pulled out his mouth organ. The song that came to him was Peter, Paul and Mary's, *Five Hundred Miles*. So he played it over and over again. And he thought to himself, "There is hope…after all."

# Chapter 71 ~ Massage

J osh showed up for his massage at exactly 9:30 the next Tuesday morning. He was surprised to find Celeste's clinic in a forested area at the end of a windy dirt road. Once inside her chalet, he began to relax. The aroma of the place was charged with the scent of vanilla, and there was soft Indian meditation music playing in the background.

"Hello, Josh, how are you?" asked Celeste as she poked her head out from behind a beaded curtain.

Just fine, Celeste, it's so good to see you again. How was your Mexican Retreat?"

"It was absolutely fabulous! After all that meditation and delicious vegetarian food, I came away feeling as peaceful and calm as the Buddha himself.

"Wow—sounds wonderful—can we talk about this in more detail later?"

"Yes, but for now, come inside this cubicle and take off your clothes to prepare for your massage. You can leave your underwear on or take them off—whichever you choose.

Josh then took all his clothes off and lay down over the long, soft table on his stomach. He put his head into the open cushioned hole at the front of it and pulled a sheet over himself. The music calmed him down and made him relax completely.

Celeste entered the massage room dressed in a white smock. She slowly rubbed hot olive oil into her hands and pulled the sheet back, exposing Josh's bare back, buttocks, legs and feet. She then worked on his body for forty-five minutes—kneading the contracted soreness out of every one of his stiff joints and muscles. Again, he felt subtle electric explosions going off everywhere she touched him. Her hands were magical. When she'd covered the whole of that side of his body, she said,

"You can slowly turn over now."

Josh rolled onto his back, exposing his full nakedness.

"Oh, I see you're aroused, Josh. I've never seen a penis that large before—it'll be hard to avoid."

"Just do your best," he replied.

As she massaged his neck, shoulders and chest, Josh slipped into an ecstatic state. He was very sexually stimulated, but at the same time, calm and clear of mind. He was determined not to ejaculate.

Celeste rubbed his thighs and legs thoroughly. At the top of each of her strokes, she moved her hands under his testicles; the back of her fingers rubbed up against them. This made his passion almost explode, but he was able to hold himself in the end.

"That was fabulous, Celeste. I feel totally relaxed—maybe moving into a small satori."

"A satori would be nice for you right about now," she responded.

Once back in the lobby, she asked him,

"Josh, how are your wife and baby?"

"I think they're fine, but I haven't seen either of them for over three weeks."

"Why is that?"

"Well, when I found out that the baby was fathered by my best friend, our marriage ended pretty quickly, and I moved into a motel by myself."

Just then, another client entered the premises, so Celeste said,

"I can't talk right now but let's get together and finish this conversation sometime soon."

"Yes, sounds like a great idea. May I take you out to dinner this Friday night?"

"Yes, yes, you can. That'd be just fine."

# Chapter 72 - Romance

Josh chose a classy Italian restaurant for his first date with Celeste. He picked her up in the vehicle once owned by his father-in-law that had become his by default after Sarah was given their condo. The meal was highlighted by long white candles emanating a warm hue and two bottles of expensive French wine. The setting was very romantic. It didn't take Josh long to confirm his initial impression that Celeste was indeed a 'kindred spirit'. They shared interests in spirituality, physical fitness, sex, and a love of flowers and plants—which helped explain why they could talk for hours without experiencing the slightest elements of boredom.

"What did you learn at the Mexican Retreat?" Josh asked her.

"Many things, but the most important is simply this—there's no such thing as a personal, separate self."

"How do you mean?"

"After long periods of meditation and silence, you come to realize that your ego is nothing more than mental activity. Thoughts, feelings, perceptions and sensations are all streaming in and out of consciousness—all coming and going perpetually—and you can notice them, first arising and then disappearing. But who we really are never comes or goes and can't be an entity."

"What is it then?"

"Pure, non-objective awareness," she stated confidently. But I'll explain more about that later. Tell me about your ex-wife."

"Celeste, I had a tumultuous relationship with Sarah Sutherland for over two years. She's a powerful, attractive woman but had no interest in real spiritual matters, physical fitness or exploring the full nature of sexual activities. She was simply not adventurous in that way. We broke up, and I went to Mexico for a vacation. Just as things were coming together for me, she wrote to me, virtually demanding marriage due to her pregnancy. She neglected to tell me that the baby's father could also have been Bruce McGill—my best friend. So, my 'romantic' relationship with her is now over for good."

"Wow, Josh, that's quite a story. I'm sorry to hear it didn't work out with her. But it's strange that your interests are so close to mine. I'm a runner and a meditator—and I love sex."

"Did you say a runner?"

"Yes—I run in marathons and train for them regularly."

"Can I tell you about my experience with *inner running*?"

"Yes, I'd love to hear all about it."

After he'd gone into a full explanation of meditative running, he asked her,

"Are you married, Celeste?"

"No, I'm not. I've been living common law with a member of the folk band Sanga for four years, but we broke up when I went to the Meditation Retreat in Mexico. Meditation was not one of his interests. I'm now renting a two-bedroom condo in Tupperton, living all alone."

"Have you ever heard of tantric sex?"

"Yes, I think so, but I only understand it intellectually."

"Well, I studied under a tantric master of sorts and learned a great deal about it from her. The important thing to understand is that sex can be a path to the divine if performed with love, discipline and skill."

"Really?"

"Yes."

Celeste then leaned over the table and smiled warmly at Josh as she said,

"I'd love to learn more."

# Chapter 73 ~ Openings

After their first date, Josh and Celeste started seeing each other every day. They ran together, ate together and even began meditating together.

"Tell me all about your novel, Josh," she said one day after a long run.

"It's coming along really well now."

"What's it about?"

"It's about a mature, female healer who goes on many spiritual adventures. But the main theme is how she transforms lust into presence, finding a way to the sacred through sex."

"How does she do *that*?"

"She waits until feelings of love arise in her for men or women, and then she moves into meditative sexual activities. During her sexual experiences, she is constantly striving to open up all her chakras."

"What happens when all her chakras are opened?"

"If the proper techniques are used, and her visualizations are effective, her sexual energies are converted to spiritual power. That power can heal people. But in the immediate aftermath of sacred sex, she is thrust into the present moment in such a way that time disappears. Time is then revealed as a non-reality created by her ego."

"I'd love the idea and would like to support you in the writing of this book. And I'm wondering, would you like to transform your sexual energies into presence, Josh?"

"Yes."

"Do you have any love feelings for me?"

"Yes, very much so. Your beauty and soul have captured me completely."

"Would you like to begin experimenting sexually with me?"

"Yes."

"How shall we begin?"

"First, I'd like to fast for a few days while we continue our 'inner running'. Then I'd like to meditate with you and do some exercises to reveal how powerful the connection can be with ourselves and a cactus. *Are you willing to join me?"*

*"Yes."*

"Then, when shall we start?"

"I say tomorrow morning."

"Would you like to sleep at my place tonight then?"

"Yes," replied Josh, and here's a book to start reading."

He then went out to his car and brought her back a copy of Cleo's *Finding Nirvana Through Sex*, and said,

"This book will give you great insights and a whole new perspective."

"Thank you, Josh—I'll start reading it right away."

# Chapter 74 ~ Money

Josh slept in Celeste's spare bedroom that night and slept well. In the morning, he joined her for glasses of cold mango juice before they went on a 5 km run.

"Let's try counting our breaths on the way out and then run effortlessly on the way back."

"Okay, sure."

They ran down the block and into a meadow that led around a small lake. It was still very early in the morning, and the sun was just rising above the hills as they finished. Josh spontaneously hugged Celeste and said,

"Now, doesn't that make you feel alive—and very present?"

"Yes, it sure does," she replied, gasping for air. "Now we can start a new day on the right foot."

Then they showered, dressed, and both headed their separate ways to work.

"See you later tonight, Celeste."

"Yes."

During the day, Josh got a call from Bruce.

"Can I buy you supper tonight? I've just got to talk to you."

"Sure," replied Josh.

Then he sent a text to Celeste—

*Celeste—*

*I'm going to dinner with Bruce tonight. See you later in the evening.*

*Josh*

They ended up at a fast-food joint, and Bruce ordered a deluxe burger and fries. Josh had a cup of black coffee, steaming hot.

"Josh, how have you been doing?"

"Just fine, buddy. I'm now dating a new girl."

"Really, how's that working out?"

"Great, so far."

"That's super, my friend. Look, something's happened in my life, and I've got to share it with you."

"What's that?"

"Sarah and I have been seeing each other, and we're really getting along well."

"Have you been making love to her?"

"Yes, and she's asked me to move into her place."

"Do you want to?"

"Yes, I hope you don't mind."

"No, I don't mind."

"Josh, I'd like to buy into her place, and I've saved $48,000 to do it with. I'd like to give you that money because you bought the place originally. Then both Sarah and I will be on the title, and I'd have at least a little investment in something."

"That's not necessary, Bruce."

"Please, it's the only fair thing to do. You're still going to be out a lot of money."

"If you insist, then," said Josh. "How do you like being a father?"

"I love it."

"Seems like everything's worked out for the best, then."

"I think so."

On the way out of the burger joint, Josh sent Celeste a quick text message.

*Celeste—*

*I'll be home in twenty minutes—please wait up for me.*

*Josh*

# Chapter 75 ~ Flowering

"Looks like I'm coming into of bit of money, Celeste," Josh mentioned as soon as he got home.

"Where's that coming from?" She responded.

"Bruce and Sarah are now a couple, and he wants to buy into her place. He felt that since I'd given it to her, I should get something back. He does have heart, you know."

"How exciting!"

"Yes."

"Shall we go into a meditation?"

"Yes."

By this time, Josh had brought his green cactus over to Celeste's home and placed it beside her fireplace.

"Let's try a cactus connection contemplation. Just think about this organism. It can sit for days in searing desert heat without wilting--just being itself—calm, peaceful and fully alive. It can turn a wasteland full of wild beasts into a paradise for itself. Maybe it can teach us something."

"Josh, I'm starting to really appreciate your cactus already, but it's awfully hot in here right now. Why don't we take our clothes off for this exercise?"

"An excellent idea, my dear."

Celeste then slipped off her tracksuit and knelt on the carpet facing the cactus directly. Josh was stunned by her beauty. Her breasts were the size of medium watermelons, and her skin was flawless and pure chocolate brown. Her waist tapered into a very narrow diameter, and her legs and feet were perfectly proportioned.

"You're gorgeous, Celeste. How can I concentrate on this meditation with you sitting beside me like that?"

"You aren't so ugly yourself, but let's just concentrate on the plant, for now."

"I'll try."

Three candles illuminated the room in dim but mellow light. They both sat in silence, gazing at the cactus for several minutes before Josh began to speak in a soft voice.

"Imagine attaching hoses from our body's right into the cactus."

After a few more minutes, she replied,

"I've done that now and feel connected to it."

"Okay, now visualize pure spring water flowing between us in a circle through the plant. Do you see it?"

"Yes."

"Now pour feelings of love and compassion into the veins that connect us."

They then sat in silence, doing this visualization for over an hour. During that time, their hungry bodies flowed with loving vibrations in complete synchronicity with the cactus.

"I feel so peaceful and calm right now," she whispered.

"Me too—can I give you a massage? He said, after staring at her for a few moments.

"Yes, I'd love that."

At that point, Celeste got up and walked mindfully into her bedroom and lay face down on the edge of her bed. Josh followed and stood beside her. He then began to slowly move his hands over her back, arms, legs and buttocks. His massage was done with immense sensitivity and care. Eventually, she fell into an ecstatic sleep, so Josh just lay down beside her and drifted off himself.

In the morning, he got up early and walked through the living room towards the kitchen. As he glanced at the cactus, he exclaimed,

"Oh my God—it's covered in beautiful red flowers. Just then, he heard Celeste behind him gasping,

"That's incredible. I feel so full of joy right now. The beauty of those flowers is overwhelming.

"Yes, it sure is," responded Josh.

# Chapter 76 ~ Alive

They sat down to a breakfast of cold lemon juice sprinkled liberally with Stevia powder and then started talking.

"How long is our fast going to last, Josh?"

"Today is the last day of this program, so hang in there. Why don't we finalize our bodily purity program with a deep meditation tonight?"

"Josh, I'd like you to start sleeping in my bed."

"That would be my pleasure."

"Will you make love to me tonight?"

"Of course—and why don't we transmute sex into a tantric meditation?"

"That sounds wonderful," my darling, she responded.

Josh then left for work and thought of nothing all day but sleeping with his new love. He simply couldn't get his mind off images of her nude body. By the time he got home, he was craving sex.

"Let's not wait, Celeste. I feel like going to bed with you right now."

"That's a fabulous idea. Let me shower and get into the sack—you can join me in twenty minutes."

"That'll be great."

Josh sat down in the living room and started gazing at the exquisite cactus sitting next to her fireplace. He sat there in deep contemplation for half an hour.

"That's such a healthy, happy, alive plant," he thought.

Just then, Celeste called out,

"You can join me now."

He walked slowly into her room and stared at her jet black hair, strewn over an entire satin pillow. Her beautiful face was smiling at him.

"The basic idea of tantric sex is to transmute sexual activity into sacred acts using discipline and visualizations," he whispered.

"How does that work in practice?"

"It's fairly simple for me. All I have to do is be fully present, move slowly and enter the pleasure without releasing any sexual fluids. And I have to go through a visualization process my teacher taught me."

"What about me?"

"The same applies to you."

Josh then turned off the lights and slipped under the covers. He began to touch Celeste's softness with intense sensitivity. Her body was warm and open as Josh gently touched her breasts and stomach, caressing them carefully and putting his full attention into his hands. When he reached her pubic area, he found it soaking wet.

"Josh, I can't stand this. Please put your penis into me; I'm going crazy."

He began to visualize the golden ball moving up his spine as he entered her. Due to his size, it took him time to fully penetrate her passage. When he was inserted entirely, she groaned.

"Oh my God, I'm coming."

He waited and held his breath as Celeste exploded all over his phallus. By the time she stopped moaning, the golden ball was near his head. At that moment, he saw a strange picture in his head. It was an image of the black bull, and its horns were gigantic. It even had a burning, hairy goatee. He wrapped that picture with waves of love and immense compassion, and slowly, very slowly—it disappeared. His head was now full of light.

"Where's that amber light coming from, Josh?"

"Shhh--I love you, Celeste," he whispered into her right ear.

"I love you too, Josh. But please stay inside me longer—I'm in pure ecstasy."

Josh held himself in her for thirty more minutes and allowed his love for her to merge with the ball of light in his head. When he did finally pull out, he was still rock hard but completely dry.

"Kiss me, Josh."

At that point, he put his lips onto hers and their tongues intertwined for over five minutes. Waves of intense love poured over them and through them. They became one being. After lying together for a while, enveloped in a cocoon of love, they began to speak.

"I had three orgasms, honey, but you didn't have any."

"That's why I'm in a state of bliss right now—fully integrated into the present moment and absolutely peaceful.

"What's that like?"

"It's like being in heaven. Everything is absolutely perfect just the way it is."

After they showered and dried themselves, Celeste exclaimed,

"Wow—look at my rhododendron! It was almost dead yesterday, and now it's green and fully alive again. There's even a new bud opening up on it. How could that happen?"

# Chapter 77 ~ Healing

Celeste, my tantric guru told me that if all my chakras were ever opened through sacred sexual activity, it could lead to the healing of other beings.

"How could that possibly happen?"

God is always fully present, sending His healing energy out just as the sun constantly sends out rays of light. But worldly living appears to block that energy just the way clouds seem to block the light of the sun—and the heavier one's sins, the darker the clouds.

"I wonder if we could somehow help my Dad this way?

"What's the matter with your father?"

"He's got COPD and has to have a machine inserted into his nose to give him a constant supply of oxygen so he can breathe freely."

"I don't know, but we could try."

For the next month, Josh and Celeste made love every single night—but they did it with a difference—and a higher purpose. They did it consciously. Their goal was to transmute lust into divine activity by opening up each of their seven chakras. To do this, they worked on touching each other with extreme mindfulness, refraining from any kind of orgasm and visualizing the golden ball exercise. They also raised the quality of their diets, fasted periodically and kept up with their inner running. Josh continued working on his solitary confinement exercises.

Their love-making began to heighten their feelings of love for each other. Josh became incredibly sensitive to the needs of his woman. She was often able to read his thoughts. Over time, all the plants in her home became more alive, vibrant and green—and their energy frequently began to overflow--producing exotically beautiful flowers. A deep sense of peace began to descend upon them, and life generally became more harmonious.

Furthermore, Josh continued to work on his novel. By this time, it had begun to write itself. His main characters definitely had taken on lives of their own--quite independent of their creator.

In early August, Celeste again raised the subject of her father's medical condition.

"Let's do some work visualizing my Dad tonight?"

"Alright—now that would be something really noble."

Later that night, at the height of their sexual passion, they both paused and visualized Celeste's father in a whole state, that is to say, perfectly healthy. By this time, Celeste was able to make love fully without having an orgasm. She'd finally mastered the golden ball visualizations. They carried thoughts of her father's complete physical recovery into the day. After supper, she called her father.

"Hello Dad, we've missed you. How are you?"

"You won't believe it, honey. My coughing has stopped. I went to my doctor yesterday, and she said I could unplug my machine. I feel great!"

"What have you been doing differently, Dad?"

"Nothing at all."

"Why is this happening to you?"

"I don't know."

Celeste looked straight at Josh when she put the phone down and exclaimed,

"Josh, it's working."

He then sat down in the corner of the living room, took out his mouth organ, and started playing Andy Williams' tune, *The Impossible Dream.*

# Chapter 78 ~ Completion

The next day, Josh had an overwhelming urge to communicate with two special people in his life. The first email of the day was for his mother. It read—

*Dear Mom—*

*I'm so sorry I haven't contacted you for several weeks—it's just that I've been so busy. I'm working full time now and have also been spending lots of time on my novel. I've wondered, from time to time, why you didn't respond to my last note. I know you must have been devastated that Sarah and I broke up because having a grandchild was always your biggest dream.*

*But life has moved on, and this time my news is good. I've fallen in love with an amazing woman whose name is Celeste Dhaliwal. We're now living together in absolute bliss because she's so compatible with me. She's a spiritual person, a meditator and a massage therapist. We've been experimenting with techniques for healing ourselves and others, and our outcomes, so far, have been quite positive. I think of you often and wish you could visit us.*

*Love and blessings,*

*Josh*

The second was for his spiritual guide.

*Dear Father—*

*I write to tell you that my spiritual life is now fully back on track. I've met a wonderful woman, and we've been meditating together regularly. I've taught her many of your contemplative practices, and she's responded with enthusiasm to them all. The bottom line is I'm in love, and that love is continually expanding.*

*I'll be finished my novel in about a week. Would you like to read it? It incorporates many of your techniques for existential communion with the Holy Spirit.*

*Most importantly, we've been developing some spiritual healing modalities which are proving to be very effective for ourselves and others. I give you most of the credit for this because many of the techniques we're using are yours.*

*Thank you again for your unlimited support, and I pray all is going well with you and your hermitage activities.*

*Josh*

"It's strange," Celeste, "But I've never spoken to the hermit much about *theories* of healing. He doesn't intellectualize much—he just demonstrates spiritual healing by his presence and his teachings. I wonder how he'll respond to the fact that *we're* doing healing work?"

"We'll know soon, my dear. Why don't we sit down now and do some healing visualizations directed towards both your mother and your teacher?"

"Now that's a great idea, my dear."

# Chapter 79 ~ Miracles

Within two days, Josh received responses from both his mother and teacher. His mother wrote—

*Dear Josh—*

*Thank you for your thoughtful note—I was delighted to hear from you, of course. Yes, I've been depressed about your break-up with Sarah and the news that her baby wasn't yours. But I'm happy to hear you're now with a new girl who seems to be a real kindred spirit. But the main reason I haven't contacted you is that I've been very ill with double pneumonia for over a month. Nothing my doctor could do was helping. However, miraculously, I woke up yesterday completely healed—my lungs are now clean and clear. So you see—God does work in mysterious ways!*

*I've decided to take the bus and visit you for a week next month. I'll be arriving in town on September 7th and plan to stay at the Seaview Motel. Could you pick me up at 10 am at the bus depot?*

*I'm really looking forward to this trip.*

*See you soon,*

*Love,*

*Mom oxo*

Father Graham's email read—

*Dear Josh—*

*Thank you for your recent update. I'm very pleased to hear about your spiritual progress and, yes, I'd like to read your book! Can you email it to me?*

*As for your healing work, I'd like to remind you that the ministry of Jesus was characterized by physical, emotional and spiritual healings. Even a superficial reading of the New Testament will reveal that He performed many astounding miracles.*

*Your healing activities are very encouraging and on the right track. I pray you will keep them up.*

*You'll be happy to hear that just yesterday, I heard that the Mexican Ministry of Transportation is planning to pave the road from Palarta to Esoterica. This means it'll be much easier for students and colleagues to visit me! On top of that, our monastery received an internet connection this very week.*

*My prayerful love goes out to you and Celeste. May the Peace of Christ be with you both, always.*

*Father Graham*


After reading the emails, Josh shared them with Celeste.

"Do you think our visualizations and contemplations had an impact on your mother and teacher, Josh?"

"Yes, I most definitely do."

# Chapter 80 ~ Happiness

The next morning, after breakfast, Josh and Celeste gathered around their cactus and started talking.

"How do you feel about my mother coming to visit us, Celeste?"

"I feel great about it. I can't wait to meet her and get to know her."

"Are you available to pick her up at the bus depot on September 7th at 10 am? I'll be at work then."

"Yes, I'd love to."

"Okay, I'll write and tell her that you'll be waiting for her when she gets here."

Then the conversation turned to more spiritual matters. It started when Celeste shared one of her insights into authentic spirituality.

"It seems like the essence of spirituality is simply to see through the illusions of our own conditioning, and the hypnosis of worldly values, land in the eternal, timeless Now—and stay there."

"Yes," responded Josh, "and when that happens, everything is revealed as sacred and perfect—*just the way it is*."

"And I'm convinced that it helps when two or more people concentrate and integrate their spiritual practices, Josh."

"Absolutely—and we've proven that sexual activities can be harnessed and transfigured into a spiritual power that can heal."

"That's amazing."

"Celeste, I had a dream a few days ago and want to share it with you now."

"What was the dream about?"

"You and I started a healing center in Esoterica, Mexico, and I'm certain the dream was a message from God. I now believe starting such a center is God's will for us."

"I love it, Josh. We could make it a spiritual healing center but also have massage and meditation sessions made available."

"We could also possibly have access to Father Graham's enclave, Celeste."

"When you write the padre and send him your completed novel, why don't you get his input on this idea?

"I absolutely will. I'll do it right away. But first, I have a very personal question to ask you."

"What is it, Josh?"

"Celeste, I love you and just know you're meant to be my life partner. I'm so happy just being in your presence, and further, my sexual addictions have now been healed. At last, I'm in a successful intimate relationship with a woman that can be a permanent one—for the first time in my life. Here's my question: Will you marry me?"

Celeste looked deeply into Josh's eyes, and he gazed right back into hers. They sat together silently in that adoring position for over ten minutes before she clearly stated,

"Yes."

# About the Author

Kama Tarumi is a writer, a spiritual healer and a tantric master. She conducts workshops worldwide, teaching people how to heal their wounds and experience inner liberation from fear, anxiety and depression. Her techniques include meditation, contemplation and sacred sexual practices. She lives in Northern BC with her partner, Rodney Eagle Claw, and her Siamese cat, Tranquility.

www.ingramcontent.com/pod-product-compliance
Lightning Source LLC
Chambersburg PA
CBHW080822020726

47501CB00009B/2380